Wildwood Flower

James B. Cooper

Chapter One

You would think that if you spent all that money for a pair of horses and a buggy that they would be so much faster than a normal rig your travel time would be appropriately shortened. After all, you should be able to expect more for your money!

Not so with this beautifully matched pair of Bays. In spite of their synchronized gait and flowing mane, and in spite of this glinting, brass-trimmed buggy, and even though said buggy included a bump smoothing ride (the very best money could buy), the pace was too slow. We were moving along no faster than a couple of nags pulling a plow. They'd better pick it up or there would be hell to pay.

"Can't we go a little faster, Sam? At this rate he's going to be home before we get there."

"Maybe some, Missus, but not enough to make a difference." After a pause, "An' they'd be winded by the time we got back. The ol' man would've skinned me fo' shore in the old days for windin' a pair. 'Sides, Mr. Mark'll unnerstand. You been takin' care of your Ma'! She shore looked proud in that new outfit, don' she?"

"Uhh! Sure, the day Mark's understanding the sun won't come up."

With a wry chuckle, "Yeah! Still your Mamma's face makes it wurt it, don' you think?"

"Absolutely! It's just that maybe Mark'll be a little late and if we could go a little faster I could get some food on before he gets home. You know what he's like!"

The big man of undeterminable age knew all too well. He had been the brunt of that temper since Mark had been a child. Lately he was even worse than his father had been.

Sam had worked for the whole family before Mark had married and given him a job at the new place. Lost in thought he expertly snapped his whip above the matched pair's rumps and clucked to induce a pace that was quicker but still well within their comfort zone.

"Yas'um I sure do, but you just got to bear the burdens life puts on ya'. Don' do no good to keep worrin'. Ya' just got to bear up, an' keep goin'. You're strong enough an' that sure was proud you made your Ma today. Might be that's more important than what Mr. Mark thinks 'bout his suppa'."

"I know! I know, you're right! She never had a real finished dress before in her whole life. I thought she was goin' to bust. Pride had her so puffed up. Being able to do that for her should make all of us proud for a long time." She paused, "Did you see that clerk? I thought he was downright rude. The way he looked at me. I've a good mind to tell Mark about it."

"Now Missus Elsa, if you don' mind my sayin', he didn't say 'nothing. 'Bout all he did was moon over you. I tol' ya' plenty a' times what a girl as pretty as you does to a man. I mean a young man that is. Can't be really surprised that he was so discombobulated with you right there beside him."

Elsa didn't miss his attempt to backtrack, "What do you mean 'a young man'? Aren't you affected by my beauty, Sam?" She loved this. About the only way to get to the big man was to accuse him of immorality.

"Now that ain't funny, Missus Elsa. You knows I ain't lookin' at you that a'way." The tone was one of rebuff.

As usual, Elsa ignored the tone. "Well, I guess I'll just have to make myself better lookin' so's I can get the better type of man. Even though you're already takin' I can still dream!"

"Now girl you stop that. It's not nice makin' fun of a ol' man like that."

A tinkle of laughter came from the back seat. "All right. We don't want to get Mrs. Cooper jealous anyway."

After a pause, "You're right about that clerk. If it got back to my wonderful father-in-law, he would probably have him skinned or at least run out of town. I just wasn't thinking. He was just so smarmy, he gave me the creeps."

They rode in silence as they left the city of Chicago behind. You knew when the city turned to countryside. It was when the intersecting roads stopped happening every block but lengthened out to occur only at sectional lines. Even out here the houses were still plentiful because of the number of people moving out of downtown like the Daileys had done.

Sam swung the carriage onto the lane leading to their home. It was a large, plantation-style home. White and majestic-looking, set as it was in such pastoral beauty. The place had once been a source of great pride in Elsa. The colonial style architecture and picturesque surroundings had made her feel important when she remembered where she had lived before her marriage.

Now it was the holder of terror. Any discontinuity from the established norm that her husband had forced might cause great pain to her.

Thankfully, they could see that no one had been here since they had left.

"Don' think he's home yet, Ma'am."

Without a reply, they made quick work of unloading and Elsa beat a hasty path to the kitchen to prepare the evening meal. While Sam wheeled away to care for the animals.

The food was almost ready when she heard the front door opening and knew it was Mark. She had heard his horse clop by on the way to the barn several minutes ago.

"I'm home! Where are you?" He was a handsome man by everyone's account, but he was soft looking. He was going to be fat before long but while still a young man looked big and strong. His well-dressed business attire was appropriate for the son of the owner of the largest slaughterhouse and meatpacking operation in Chicago.

"In the kitchen." After he had made his way to the kitchen, "So, how was your day?"

"Lousy! That buffoon of a father of yours could not do anything right if you stood and showed him how to do his job the entire time he's at work." Mark stood lounging in the door frame, surveying the scene before him, as his beautiful wife prepared a meal.

"Why? What happened?"

"His whole line was down for two whole hours. The entire plant was at a standstill, and, naturally, Dad took it out on me. If I had a nickel for every pound of rear-end your dad has lost me since he went to work there we'd be a lot better off."

"Well, why does his line being off have to be his fault?"

"Well, it was! Said he had to turn it off to keep from piling up the hindquarters, but then he couldn't get it to start up again. If he wasn't as slow as a snail, they wouldn't have piled up in the first place."

"Well wasn't there something wrong with the line that it wouldn't turn back on and not Pa's fault?"

"Woman, I did not come home just to hear you argue with me. If I say it was so-and-so then it was dammed well so-and-so, and I will thank you to keep your mouth shut with your arguin'."

Elsa knew to let it go. The tone had turned brutal. Her husband moved his big frame toward the kitchen table. Yanking his chair out, he plopped a belligerent form into it and pulled up to the table. "What's for supper?" The tone was one of demand.

"We're having lamb tonight."

"What! What in thunderation you tryin'? That's what we had last night."

"I know. I was late getting home today and I had to get something fast. It's good! You liked it."

The words just spit out, "You'd think that if I worked myself to death, you could get the only job you have done when I get home."

The tone warned Elsa. She knew what was likely to follow that tone of voice. It had been several months since the last time, but she knew the warning signs well. She kept her back to him as she moved to a cabinet drawer and pulled it open. With her body carefully placed between Mark and the drawer she put something heavy into her apron pocket and said in an equally hostile voice.

"This is the first time in a year and a half that you've had to have leftovers and it just took longer than I thought it would to get Ma fit for her new dress." The heavy weight pulling at her apron strings reassured her.

"You been out all day runnin' around with that no-good family of yours while I have to eat crap after breakin' my back to earn the livin'?"

"It's not crap. Anyone would love to have this for their meal." Setting his plate before him and moving back. "And there is nothing wrong with my family. They are just as good as yours or even better."

"You were sure anxious enough to get away from them when I proposed to you."

"Maybe it was because I thought I loved you then. Did you ever think of that?"

He was screaming now, "Well sure as hell you don't now."

Elsa's voice dropped to a hoarse whisper, "Whose fault do you think that is?"

Mark had his arms resting on the table. His head bent, he sat motionless for several beats, and then he exploded.

Bolting upright he sent his chair careening into the hutch. Lunging around the corner of the table he was on Elsa before she could run. His big paw smashed at her lovely face.

Her arm went up to ward off the blow, but she wasn't strong enough to stop it. His fist crashed into her jaw and sent her flying across the room.

This first attempt to ward off his strike had at least managed to soften its force enough to allow her to regain her balance before Mark could close the distance to strike her again. In the past it had always been this second blow that had done her in. She was fast enough to keep his first from landing solidly, but always it hurt her enough that she was helpless against further strikes.

This time it was going to be different. Elsa had warned him last time to never hit her again. Her warning had lasted until now, but she had meant it. Mark should have realized it meant forever. Elsa put her hand into her apron pocket and shot Mark in the stomach through the cloth of her apron pocket.

Mark was moving as fast as he could after Elsa when the bullet struck him. He clutched his stomach with both hands and stumbled on for a few steps. He got his momentum stopped and looked down at his belly. Mimicking an accordion he crumpled to the floor.

Elsa pulled her hand out of her pocket with her still smoking gun attached. Mark had had it made especially for her when they were first married. Said he didn't want her out here without protection. It had been tailored to fit her hand without losing firepower. Sam had spent hours a day helping her become a marksman with it and the results of his handiwork lay on her kitchen floor. She had not missed.

Mark mumbled the words, "You've killed me!"

Elsa laid her pistol on the table and knelt beside the prone man. Turning him onto his back, she could now see the life ebb and flow out of him as too much blood spread on the floor. "Yes. You're dying." It sounded flat and unemotional.

She rose and sank into a chair at the table looking down on Mark's prone body. It was all different with Mark's crumpled form lying before her. She had until now been very matter-of-fact. The warning signs she knew so well, the preparing for the inevitable and the deed itself had all been performed with a problem-solving thought process that would have made a professor proud.

Now with Mark prone before her something jumped from her inner being into her throat. It was choking her. Sickness seemed to settle right in her throat and engulf her. Terror that even Mark had not inspired washed over her.

"Guess I had it comin', but damn I'm too young to die."

"Yes you did and yes you are." It was flat; matter of fact.

It was quiet for a few moments. "You know, I always loved you don't you? Don't know why I couldn't treat you better." The voice would not even make a hoarse whisper.

The pool around his prostrate body was getting huge. Elsa could see that his life was close to ending. "Yes, I know!" After a brief pause, "And I wish you could have too."

There were a few more moments of silence as he ebbed closer to death, before the sound of running boots hitting the front porch brought Elsa back to the present. She fought the sickness in her throat as Sam's yelling came from the front door. "You all right, Mrs. Elsa? You all right?"

The fear passed. She got up and headed to the parlor. Elsa opened the front door. "Yes Sam! I'm fine."

"Oh, thank God. I could've sworn I heard a shot. Couldn't figure anything but from here."

"Yeah, it was. I was practicing my quick draw while I was cooking and the gun went off in the kitchen."

"Oh, is that all? How many time I tell you." He scolded, "Don't do no good to be the first to level, if you ain't got it cocked to shoot. Girl you better take it slow. You'll shoot off'n you own foot if you aint careful."

Some part of her mind must have started to work because she made plans for her future. "Well thank you Sam. You're right, I'll be more careful.

I'm glad you came up. Mark said to tell you that we're going into town for the weekend. He said for you to take the rest of the day off and there's no need to come in tomorrow. You can take it off with pay and we'll see you Monday."

"Child, what's that on your face? Did he hit you again?"

"Yes, but he stopped now and everything's all right. You can go on now. Tell Mrs. Cooper I said hi."

"Yas'um." The large, black man stood looking at Elsa for some time. Noting her dis-composure, he said, "Well guess I'll be goin'. You better be careful, Missus. It can be dangerous out there."

Ignoring his insight, "Ok Sam. Oh, by the way, I'll leave your pay on the tack room desk in case we don't make it back by Monday."

She closed the door on the back of the man who was leaving. The only friend she had had since she moved here. What was she going to do now? She walked to a parlor chair because she couldn't go back into the kitchen and sank into the plush upholstery.

She could go get the sheriff but would Mr. Dailey jump in to warp everything into making her wrong. The answer was obvious. All one had to do was watch him since Mark had proposed marriage to see what he considered her. And, while he treated Mark like a dog, she had also seen what he would do if someone harmed Mark. It was an affront to him personally and he would turn deadly. No, she couldn't get the sheriff. A woman just had to put up with what her husband demanded.

That left running. Staying here was out of the question. There was a penalty for murder. So run where? There were only four directions in which to go. Maybe west. Lots of folks had been going to California. They had found gold there some years back and now a lot of people lived there.

Even that old devil would never be able to find her there. That was it wasn't it. She had to avoid that vindictive old man. He wasn't going to take this lying down. No, he would want blood for this even though he knew what Mark did to her.

That meant he would fire her father. What would her family do without him working? How could she get money to them? Sam! She could leave Sam enough in the barn to take care of his family and then trust him to take what her family needed to them. There was plenty in the safe upstairs. If the old man knew that Mark had taken that much over the years he would have shot him himself.

Well, that was it! Everything that she had ever known was here, but she couldn't stay. That's just the way it was.

She sat for a while longer to consider if there was anything else. There wasn't and Elsa wasn't one to hesitate once she decided. Only the worst of luck would get Mark's body found before Monday. That gave her four days in which she could put distance between herself and that old man. Maybe two more days before the authorities could get circulars after her.

So six days and then she would have to avoid roads and no towns. They'd play hell finding her after that.

She rose and entered the kitchen. Working around the large pool, she retrieved her gun and packed food supplies and utensils in a bag. Hauling that beside the front door, she proceeded upstairs.

There she packed a bag with road clothes and opened the safe that she'd carefully acquired the combination for by watching over a long period of time. Taking out its contents she put part of the money into two envelopes, addressed both and went downstairs. Leaving everything but the envelopes she proceeded to the barn.

She made great haste to saddle her mount and rig a packsaddle on the big black. Taking them back to the porch, she loaded the black with her bundles. In less than fifteen minutes she had embarked on her new life.

Chapter Two

Sam knew that there was something wrong. He had known it last week when Elsa had told him to take the rest of the week off, and now that he was returning to work it weighed heavily on him. He hated Mondays anyway. Two days of lying around and playing with his grandchildren spoiled him to working, especially as he got older. It was getting harder and harder to find the energy to go to the Dailey's on Mondays and this time it was infinitely worse.

As he turned off the main road and let his mount pick its way past the house and on to the barn, the feeling of foreboding grew. The feint hope that he was wrong vanished as he saw the forlorn, vacant look of the house.

Sam had watched Elsa's face as she gave her explanation for the shot he had heard last week and he had known. Not exactly what had happened but he knew that whatever had happened was not good. Now, he had to face finding out what it was and he did not like that.

Elsa was worth all the Daileys combined in Sam's book. She had proven to be honest, strong and courageous over and over again. Now, Sam was afraid she was in trouble.

When he looked at the two envelopes on his desk after tending his horse, Sam was sure of it. He had a desk in the tack room of the barn where he kept the records for the place. He had made a good living for the young Daley in the two years he had worked for him. The boy had bought good land.

Sam figured that in times past the lake had flooded up silt and made the land sandy-loam and fertile. Sam had run cattle and grown corn. He had learned to love the land as if it were a person, but looking at those two envelopes put a catch in his throat. He knew things were changing for him.

One envelope was addressed to him and the other addressed to Elsa's mother. There was no way this could be good. He opened the one addressed to him. The worst became the most probable.

There was money in it. He carefully counted the bills stuffed into the envelope. $5000! More than Sam had earned in his whole life. Oh, Elsa what have you done?

Sam had walked off a plantation in Georgia as a young man and hadn't stopped walking until he met a girl here in Chicago. She had held him here and he had gone to work for Mr. Dailey. First he had worked in the meat packing plant, then on Mr. Dailey's land. When the boy got married, the old man wanted him to work for his son and Sam had agreed. There was more money before him now than he had gotten in all those years. Now, he was forced to find out why.

He stood and placed each envelope in his front pockets. He checked his front to make sure that no bulges showed, and headed for the house. It was empty.

He could feel that emptiness but he knocked anyway. Getting the expected no response he pushed the door open. It was all Sam could do to not loose his breakfast. Only with extreme will power was he able to not throw up as the stench washed over him. He knew for sure now. Making his way into the house, Sam found Mark in the kitchen. Or at least discovered what condition he was in, because the boy sure was dead.

Sam had never felt comfortable in the house even with Elsa the only one around, so now he made his way to the barn and decided what to do next. She had killed him-probably to keep him from hitting her. Sam knew what that was like. He had felt like shooting Mark himself in the past. Seeing what Mark had done to that beautiful face, oh those many times, had made murder flare up inside him.

The missus had always counseled against it. She had told Sam that his family needed him too much for him to throw his life away by righting a wrong.

Now Sam wished he had shot the skunk because Missus Elsa was in real trouble. How was he going to handle this now?

He made up his mind that he was just going to tell the truth and trust in the Lord to sort it out. With that in mind, he saddled and went home where he left the two envelopes and talked to his wife. They decided among other things that he needed to go to the Marshall's office instead of the Sheriff's. Which was where he was now. After talking to a young man in uniform he was shown into the Marshall's office and looked at a handsome older man in uniform.

"Yes, Sir. My deputy says you have a dead body to report!"

"Yes, sir! I found my boss dead in his home when I went to work this morning."

"Well. Mr. Cooper is it? That must have been a shock to you. Have a seat and tell me about it. Where was he exactly?"

"He's in the kitchen of his house and he's been shot. Looks like."

"Who is this man?"

"His name is- or was- Mark Dailey."

"The Dailey?"

"Yes, sir! He's the son of Ken Dailey."

"That boy was married wasn't he? Was his wife around?"

"Yes, he was married, but I didn't see Missus Elsa around."

"She gone a lot?"

"No, sir. I'd say she's never gone wit' out Mark or me takin' her."

"Well, then when was the last time you saw her?"

"That'ta been last week. Must'a been Thursday. She needed to tell me Mr. Mark had told me to take the rest of the week off on'a count'a they was goin' out'a town."

"You see Dailey then?"

"No, sir, but nothin' unusual 'bout that. I'd go long times wit'out seein' him."

"What about the house? Seem to be in order or was it rearranged?"

"Not in the house much, wouldn'a gone in this morning if there hadn'a been that smell. Mostly I stay around the barn or the land, but from what I could see it looked alright."

"OK, Mr. Cooper, better show me where this body is. Tell you what. If you'll go by the morgue and get the county coroner, I'll go tell Mr. Dailey and meet you out at his place."

∞

Sam sat on the front porch away from the open front door. There were two men with him in business attire. They were the coroner and his assistant and it was they who had decided to open both the back and front door to allow the stench to blow out.

All three studied the two riders approaching. The Marshall cut a fine figure on his mount; tall, well-dressed and handsome for a man of his age. The figure next to him resembled a vulture most closely. Tall, rail-thin and with a dark, brooding face rode the elder Dailey.

Both men tied up at the hitching post in front of the house instead of going to the barn with their mounts. The three figures seated on the porch stood and walked to the front of the porch as the Marshall and Mr. Dailey strode up the walk to the house.

"Hey, Walt. Hi, Newt. Glad to see you could come out on such short notice. You looked at the body yet?"

"Marshall. Looked but we didn't touch anything. Wanted to let you see it just like it was before we really went to work."

"I appreciate that. Mr. Cooper don't remember askin' you if you touched or moved anything. Did you?"

"Opened the door and walked on the floor. Nothin' else."

"Good! Let's take a look."

Ken Dailey showed no inclination to follow them as the four men moved into the house. The open doors had done wonders for the smell but exploded the number of flies. They were swarming as the group entered the kitchen.

"Well, I don't see nothin' to say but that the body is lying on its back between the table and stove. Anybody else have something that they want noticed?" Silence followed the inquiry. "Ok, looks like a gunshot to me in the lower abdomen. You say the same thing Doc?"

"Yeah! We'll look at everything when we get him back to the morgue, but for now-gut shot! Can we have him now?"

"Have him and welcome to him. Come on Mr. Cooper, let get out of this smell and let these men do their work."

The Marshall stopped in the living room of the spacious ranch house and turned to Sam. "Let's talk about this wife. She have folks around here?"

"Yup! Got a mother and father with three sisters livin' over on the Southside. Washington Ave., Maybe the 300 block. I think that's all."

"If she was in trouble is that the only place you can think of that she would go?"

"Guess I don't think she'd go there. Only bring trouble down on her folks. No, if she did this, she took off. I'm bound to tell you that she is one wonderful person and if she did do this there was plenty of provocation. It was the last thing she could do and she did it to protect herself.

That skunk on the kitchen floor has in the past beaten her something brutal and was goin' to do it again in the future. That old man out in the front yard had him so messed up it was all that poor girl could do. A clear case of self-defense is what you'll find when this is all over."

"OK, Mr. Cooper, we'll see how it turns out. Not up to me to figure it out. That's for a judge to do. My job is to find out what happened and I need to talk to her to find that out. I really appreciate you're bein' forthright with me.

Got to say that you've been very cooperative and I admire a man that's not afraid of the truth. I'll see what I can do about finding the young lady and talkin' to her. Her side is probably very interestin'."

The two men walked out of the house to find Ken Dailey pacing in the yard. Sam knew the figure well. For over forty years they had had a close relationship, and Sam hated him. That's not to say that he did not respect him.

Sam knew how Daley had managed to accumulate his powerful position. His scrawny frame told only part of the story. You had to look at the broad shoulders and appreciate the long levers of his arms and legs to accurately access the man's physical power.

His energy was what Sam really did not understand. He was always working. That drive was what had put him where he was but it also made him a despicable human. Sour, overbearing, and ruthless were the traits which that drive also fostered. He was obviously worked up now and Sam held back, letting the Marshall lead.

"You got this figured out now?"

"Well, it's your son and he's dead. Been gut shot and he's lyin' in the kitchen of his own house. Sure sorry about your loss. Let me ask if you know anyone who would do this?"

"What! You've got to be kiddin'. That filthy, gutter-trash of a girl did this. No question about it! You need to arrest her dead or alive. I can't tell how many times I've warned that boy to leave her. She's a gold-digger of the first order but she had him blind.

Tried to tell him that you do'nt' marry gutter trash like that. Keep her on the side and marry a woman worthy of your own status. No way he would listen. Now see where it got him. He never listened to me and now he's paid the price.

I want that woman hung for what she's done and it's your job to see it gets done."

"I appreciate your input on this matter and I understand your loss but I know what my job is. Mr. Cooper says he beat her. You know anything about that?"

"That's a lie, a god-damned lie. Mark would never do anything like that. You, you stinkin' nigger, you get your stuff and get off my property. I see you ever again and I'll personally horse whip ya'." He was beyond reason and the tone of his voice was hysterical.

Sam paid him no attention. Sam had always had something dangerous about him. It was more than his still powerful build that old age failed to erase and the grace with which he moved. An unaccompanied black man in the slave states and many adjoining states would be detained and returned as property. While Sam deliberately encountered as few people as possible on his long walk from Georgia, no one detained or challenged him on this long road to freedom. That was as sober a testament to his inapproachability as possible.

Even now, in spite of his lowly status in the community, no one had ever tried to push him beyond what seemed prudent, and he knew that this would be no different. Ignoring Me Dailey, he slowly turned to face the Marshall, "You need me anymore, sir?"

"No, Mr. Cooper. If I need you, I'll look you up. You're free
 to go now with my high regard."

"Well guess I'll be goin' then." Sam turned and walked off toward the barn.

He had already decided to just saddle his horse. He could get his stuff tomorrow or the next day when everyone was not around. The assistant was hitching up his team to the wagon when he got to the barn. They exchanged greetings and Sam turned his mount out to the lane, out of his work place for the last few years. Mr. Dailey and the Marshall were still talking in the yard when he went past.

Sam and his wife had decided earlier that the envelopes meant that Elsa was gone. Sam decided now that the Marshall would have to return to Chicago and alert the Sheriff about going to Elsa's parents to look for her.

The Marshall was in charge of Cook County and the Sherriff was in charge of the city limits. That would give Sam time to go home, get Elsa's parent's envelope and take it to them before any law showed up. He could let them know what had happened and prepare them for the law's visit. Let Elsa's father know not to go back to work.

After he had accomplished that, there would be nothing left for him to do but kick back and enjoy what Elsa had given his family. Sam was ashamed to think how easy it was going to be for him and how hard it was going to be for that girl. He was only solaced by the thought that she was tough enough to take it.

Chapter Three

She had held to her plan. Not that she thought it was the only plan or that no other plan could compare, but because she just did not know any better. How law enforcement worked was beyond her ken. It was the best guess she could make from a position of absolute ignorance. She had no idea what law enforcement did.

So she followed her original plan to the letter. The first six days were spent traveling along well maintained roads. She and her mounts made very good time. The mare and stallion were not used to being ridden and packed all day, every day, but they were bred to it and after a few days, showed no ill effects. She had brought oats for the horses and therefore had no need to let them graze.

For herself, Elsa got over saddle soreness quickly and was able to get by with only snatches of sleep. She had laid waste to all her hopes and dreams and been forced to strike out into the vast unknown. The need for sleep had deserted her, so they stopped for a couple of hours twice daily and the rest of the time they traveled.

At the end of her self-imposed six days, they had traveled a long way. They had left Illinois behind and were well into Iowa. They had stayed on the roads and gone as fast as the animals could travel. Now, they had to avoid anyone seeing them.

Since then they had traveled well off the road but in a parallel direction. This sometimes made going very slow but it also resulted in solving her food problem. Elsa had brought along her hand gun, a rifle, and a shot gun. The rifle she still could not hit anything with. She had taken several shots at deer and antelope but had hit nothing. The shotgun was a different story.

At first, the mare did not like having it go off just over her head, but she soon reconciled herself to the noise when she decided that it would not hurt her. They would kick up several covey of quail just about every morning. Pheasant and turkey were encountered less often but lasted longer. This mastery of the shotgun provided birds to Elsa's fill. Now she had a problem with staples. She was out of flour. The last small amount had weevils in it and she had to throw it out. All her vegetables were used up except for part of a potato and one carrot. No matter the danger she was going to have to stop.

Many of the rivers she had crossed had forced her to return to the road and cross over the bridge. She had done so very carefully and had not been seen once that she knew of.

The last time she had done this, there had been a sign saying that the town of Sioux City was just ahead and she had decided to stop there. She had made a plan. She thought it best to skirt the town and enter from the east. That way, no one would know she was traveling west if they remembered her at all.

She also decided to arrive in the early morning hours so she could bundle up to conceal her figure as she rode in. She was going to tell the store keeper that her husband was sick and could not come in himself.

That was the plan and the plan accounted for her appearance as she let her mount walk at her own pace down the dusty road. Bundled in her Mackinaw, with her hair stuffed into her hat, she slouched in the saddle until they pulled up before what had to be the general store.

Her self-image was one of a tramp, dirty from the trail, just pulling into town. In truth her clothes were too expensive and her mounts were too spectacular. No one had ever seen a pack horse the equal of the Black and her mare was Arabian.

There were only two groups of people around at this hour but they noticed her figure and beauty when she stepped down and walked into the store. The only place Elsa could have hidden was in a beauty contest among other women as lovely as she was.

Of course she did not know this and walked into the store with all the confidence that she was pulling her deception off.

"Howdy ma'am. What can I do for you this beautiful morning?"

He was a tall skinny man, with unusually large hands.

"I need some staples. My husband and I are about out of everything. We need flour, potatoes, whatever else you have for fresh vegetables and do you have any fruit?"

"Just canned but I have some cucumbers just in and some beautiful tomatoes."

The idea of tomatoes was the most exciting thing Elsa had heard in a month. "Oh, that sounds great. I'll take as many as won't spoil for the next week. Plenty of potatoes, some carrots if they're good, and a slab of pork back, also. Canned fruit will be all right. Do you have peaches?"

"Sure do. Some cherries too, if you want them."

"Oh, that sounds great!" Elsa's stomach was going to start cramping at just the thought.

The store keeper hustled about his business. Calling out goods as Elsa gave instructions on each, "Say your husband's around? You don't mind my askin', why's he not here? Not good for a young lady to be unaccompanied in these parts."

"He's out at our camp. He got sick yesterday, and I made him sleep while I came in to get these. He says it's my cookin' that made him sick
but he sure has got the maladies.

We'll probable pull on through town tomorrow, but we were out of so much I decided to come in today and get what we need. Might be pullin' through before you'all get up."

"Like to get a early start do ya'? Cain't say as I blame ya'. Getting' hot lately.   Better to rest in the afternoon." He was totaling up the bill and gathered up her order when she had paid.

Carrying it to her pack, he loaded her items in and stepped back to allow her to mount. "Sure a fine lookin' pack animal ya' got there Missus. You must be real proud of him!"

"He's my husband's mount, but he packs just fine. Thanks for all your help. Hope I see you in the morning. Might need some more things when we pull through."

"You take care Missus. It was a pleasure see'n you. Come back anytime."

Elsa could not help it. She had been a beautiful woman her whole life, and therefore was used to being looked at. If she'd been normal, she might have noticed the unusual attention a group of men paid her as she rode by them for a second time. She did not notice.

To her there was nothing unusual going on at all. You can say she was stupid. That she was in a precarious position, and should have been paying better attention. Certainly her life would have been different if she had, but you have to understand that we can only be what we are!

∞

Her eyes were wide open and she was reaching for her pistol before she knew what was going on. About the time her hand touched the leather
of an empty holster, she became aware of a group of men standing around her. She had made her blankets with her head toward a tree and there were men ringing her except for the space occupied by the tree.

"Howdy, Ma'am. Thought you might sleep all night."

The voice came from a man standing at her feet that resembled a bear in the dim light from the dying camp fire. He had on a buffalo coat in spite of the warm night. That bulk, the black beard and dirty hair made the impression of a black bear complete.

Elsa was later to decide that he wore the robe to make himself look bigger and the greasy appearance of the entire man was just for added appeal. "Who invited you into my camp?"

"Well, no one strictly speakin'. We was just passin' and decided to be neighborly. You don't sound like you're glad to see us?"

"I'm certainly not. You need to all leave before my husband gets back."

Oh! Where would that husband of yours be?"

"He just went out to relieve himself and he'll be right back."

"Must be a long pee he needs. We been followin' you for a couple of days and haven't seen hide nor hair of him."

"Well, he'll be right back and you better leave before he does."

"I don't think so little lady. I think we's the only men around to take care of you. I think we better see that you don't get hurt or anything."

Elsa was terrified. Her life had been uncomfortable before, now it was dangerous and she could not think of anything to do. "What did you do with my gun?" She demanded.

The big man ignored her, "What in the world are ya' doin' out here on this prairie by yourself? Must be in a world of hurt."

"That's none of your business. You need to go and leave me alone. I wasn't doing anything to hurt you, so get out of my camp!"

A growl came from her right side as the man standing there spoke up, "What're we waitin' for? Let's get on with it!"

"You're waitin' on me, Wes. So shut you're stupid mouth and wait."

Paying no more attention to Wes as he would a fly, the big man turned back to Elsa. "Come on little lady, what's ya' doin' out here? You runnin' from the law?"

"That's none of your business. You need to leave."

"No, we like it here. Might stay a long time."

Elsa had been sitting up since she found her gun gone and now realized there was no mercy to be shown. She aimed a kick with all her might at the big man's knee. He moved and she missed as he reached down and pinned her legs to the ground.

"Get her arms." He commanded, as he shifted his weight to kneel, and use the weight of his knees on Elsa's thigh to pin her to the ground. Strong hands forced her back into a laying position, and strong hands ripped at her shirt. The bear kneeling on her leg undid her dungarees. With one mighty pull he had them down to her thighs and she felt the last remnants of her garments leave her upper torso. In a matter of minutes, she was left prone, naked and helpless. Trapped by power she could not hope to resist.

It was really strange to Elsa. These men were having her without her permission and inflicting a great deal of pain while doing so, but she was filled with thinking about how helpless she had been to ward off any part of it.

She had always thought that no one could rape her. She had always seen herself fighting off any unwanted advances with her strength and fury. Protected by her righteousness.

As a young girl, her friends had talked about this and they had all agreed, "Not in my back yard." They all saw themselves throwing a well-placed elbow or putting a strong kick into their adversary and thus vanquishing him to the realm of inconsequential. None of that proved possible.

Sure there were four of them and sure that made it easier for them, but Elsa had to admit that it would have made no difference in the outcome if there had only been one. There was really nothing she could have done.

This deflating fact bored into her and, when it mingled with the pain and humiliation of what was happening to her, she had doubts about her ability to go on.

They were finished and had tied her hands behind her back and bound her feet. They threw a blanket over her prone body, and retired to the built-up camp-fire to smoke and gloat.

Elsa could not get comfortable. She was forced to lie on her stomach because her hands and arms were behind her, but the skinny old man with bad teeth and breath that would gag a maggot had squeezed her left breast so hard that it still throbbed with fierce pain. She was forced to lie on her shoulder and chest on her right side to avoid that pain. There was going to be very little sleep tonight; maybe not any night for the rest of her life. What was she going to do about that?

Elsa was nothing if not a planner. The idea popped into her mind that maybe she could make them jealous of each other. She could try to make the big man think she had fallen in love with him and could not live without him. It sounded stupid on the face of it, but if she started making him think that he was just so much man that the others were no good in comparison, he might assert himself to make them leave her alone. She could then work on getting him to trust her and provide a means of escape.

Might not be the best plan in the world but it held out a course of action that let her at least picture salvation. She would hold on to that, and try to get some sleep.

Chapter Four

The town had grown! There was a time when the major ranches were the only support and the reason for its existence. Now, there were farms sprouting up along the many creeks in the area and the town merchants were starting to make money. The farms spent for entire families and the new businesses needed lots of equipment. They were causing a boom. The town was on a north-south road, along a tributary that dumped into the Platte down south. If you went about fifty miles north you could hit the Tyber Pass road into Montana Territory and south about five miles was the road from Chicago into Cheyenne.

Spud had stopped for a short time in the town and had then pulled out heading north. He and a helper from town had pulled off the trail into the cemetery after about a mile. It was a pretty place, situated upon a hill overlooking a part of the creek with some nice trees. This was the reason he was here.

Skinny had remembered it from his childhood. It was a well-tended cemetery. Someone had put up a one-strand fence to keep the cattle out. It had been recently scythed and, in contrast to most of the countryside around it, had a pastoral look instead of waving grass hip high. Spud had always figured that if a town took care of the graveyard, there was at least one good person living there and this one was well taken care of. Skinny had wanted to come back here and, when he knew for sure he was a goner, had begged Spud to bring him here.

The wagon was parked under a huge Cottonwood on the creek side of the hill and Spud was soon standing, working, in a chest deep hole.

He wasn't big. Course he wasn't small either. Solid might be the best way to describe him. He was almost twenty-two now. He and Skinny had met almost seven years ago and had been pards since.

Old man Wells had hired him when he came walking in with all he owned on his back. Back then his father had been leaving the farm and moving to the city. He had given both his sons the option of going with him or taking part of the proceeds from the farm and go on their own. So far Spud had walked to Texas from Ohio.

In cow country a man on foot with a backpack was unusual, but the old man was most impressed because he had a tent. Why Mr. Wells liked that, no one but Mr. Wells ever knew but he told Skinny to make a cowman out of him and everyone said he'd done a good job.

Spud had his shirt off and you could see the big muscles in his chest and shoulders work as he swung the pick to loosen up the bottom of the hole he was digging. Being a cowman had made him powerful and when combined with a heart of gold made him an admirable person by everyone's judgement.

The old man he had picked up in town was sitting by the wagon leaning against a wheel and watching the kid. "Sure wish I could help more but the pain jus' won' let me. You're too young to know but old age can be terrible."

"Hey, I didn't hire you to do anything except help me put the load in the ground. You'd be doing more than I'm paying you for if you helped me dig too. So don't worry, I'll make you earn your keep in just a little bit."

"Yeah! Sure wish I could help ya' if'n I didn't hurt so much. Fell off'n a horse some years ago and the pain is somethin' awful. Doc says I'm all busted up inside. Folks around here don' unnerstan' what happens when you hurt all the time. More than a real man can stand, I'll tell you!"

"Did you used to work cattle?"

"Yup, my whole life. Worked for the Bar B most of my life- til my terrible accident. Had to live in town since. Not like bein' out in the open. I can tell you."

Picking up the shovel to toss out the loosened dirt, "I guess not. Can't make much of a living all cooped up there?"

"Oh, just odd jobs now and then. Not enough to keep body and soul together. Folks think I drink too much but they don't know how hard it is."

"Well, I'm thinkin' you need to walk in the other man's shoes to judge him. Besides, what's important is how you treat people, and no matter what you do to yourself you can still treat other people right."

"Yeah, that's right and you won't find me abusing anyone! Treat ever' body with respect, I does."

"That's what counts!"

"Wished some folks in town could hear you say that. They's some who pass judgment without even knowin' what's what."

Spud had studied the man on the ride out to the cemetery and judged that he just needed sympathy. "You just need to ignore them. There's always some. I think this is about right if I get the loose out and shape the sides. Why don't you get one horse hitched up and back the wagon up closer over there so we can unload him near the grave."

"You don't want both of them hooked up."

"No. We're goin' to use one of them to help us put him in. One should be plenty to just maneuver the wagon around. Use the closest one, he's easier to handle and we'll need the other to help us."

The shabby old man rolled to his side and got on his hands and knees. By holding to the wagon he managed to stand upright and after getting his balance he straightened up with great effort then shuffled over to the grazing horses. Spud watched the old man and decided that he wasn't kidding about being in pain. His heart went out to the old boozer.

Maybe that was his future. He had been wondering about what the future would look like ever since Skinny had gone. Spud climbed out and the old man had the wagon just right. The coffin was long enough to set down on one end while the other was still on the wagon. By swinging the end in the wagon around, it was on the ground and Spud drug it over to where he had looped a rope around the nearby cottonwood.

He put the coffin down on top of the two loose ends of his rope and surveyed his handiwork. The rope was looped around the tree with the bitter ends trailing back over the grave. With the coffin placed upon the trailing ends, all was ready.

"Bring the other horse over and we'll tie the loose ends of the rope to him and let him pull. I figure that'll take most of the weight off and let us lower her right down into place."

After the old man had the animal in place and pulling on the rope, Spud slid the coffin down the ropes and over the grave.

By backing up the horse slowly the coffin was lowered into the grave while Spud sat on the edge and kept the coffin from rolling over.

"That's the gol'durndest thing I ever seed," as he watched Spud pull his rope from under the box and slowly coil it up. The old man moved the horse to the wagon, "you must be some kind of honcho to come up with idees like that, young fellow. Are you working around here?"

As he rummaged in his knapsack and pulled out the bible his mother had given him, "No. I don't know what my plans are when this is finished. Told my gal back home it might take a year to get back. Guess I'm faced with a choice of see'n if I can find winter work here or head on back to Texas. I guess Mr. Wells will give me work for the winter down there when I get back. Hard to get work this time of year!"

As he hooked the harness up to the singletree, the old man said, "It is hard to get work now. Everybody has their winter crew on and they's hunkerin' down for the blow."

"Must get cold up here in the winter."

"Sure can. But it don't stay real cold for long. It's not like Texas, I bet."

"Ain't nothin' like Texas, but this place looks like it has plenty of grass?"

"You bet! We're get'n more cows all the time too."

"It's kind of dry where I am. Looks like you get more rain here."

"Plenty, it got dry back in '51. We had good water ever year since then. You know if you're lookin' to stay for the winter you might look at the Rafter W. Pete Harper out there broke his leg last week and they might need another hand. Tell Mr. Wilson that I said you was ok if you'd like."

Spud standing at the head of the grave finding his place in the Bible, "Well thank you kindly, maybe I'll do that. See what you folks are so proud of around here. It can be good to find new ways." Spud found the Psalms that he liked and read it slowly with a fine voice and resolute manner.

Folding the book back he spoke with feeling "The best man except for my Pa that I ever knew or will ever know. So long Skinny, I'll sure miss you!"

Laying the book down and reaching for the shovel, Spud moved to finish the job and it wasn't long before the mismatched pair was perched on the wagon seat and headed back to town.

"Do you think your friend went to heaven? Just wonderin'."

Spud threw a glance toward the old man and changed his evaluation of him again, "Don't really know. Ma said there was a heaven and lots of folks say so now, but I don't know where it is. If it's somewhere you can bet old Skinny would be there but would that mule-head that killed him be there too. Nobody says.

For me, seems like they might just be wishful thinking. You know, it sounds good but a lot we just don't know. Is that tree going to heaven when it dies? It sure is better looking than me and never did anybody any harm so it deserves to go if any of us do. Maybe everything goes and we just don't know it. It sure would be hard to figure it all out without ever seeing it an' all. I hope ol' Skinny is there but I just don't know."

The old man offered, "So, you say you've got a women waitin' back home. Bet she's a pretty one?"

"She sure is! Makes a man feel funny just to look at her, and she's real sweet too."

"Knew you'd be a ladies man. I always liked them that knew their place and kept quiet."

"Then you'd like her. Most of the time I got to push just to get her to tell me how she feels about anything. Got a good head on her shoulders when she'll talk about things."

They rode in silence both in their own thoughts the short distance back to the town. Pulling up in front of the general store, Spud said, "Could you return the pick and shovel for me and here's your pay for the day." He placed a full dollar in the old man's hand even though he had offered him only two bits. "Good luck to you and thanks for all your help."

"Glad to help and you don't know how bad I need the money. Thanks young feller and good luck to you. Don't forget the Rafter W and so long."

The old man shuffled away, carrying the borrowed implements back to the undertaker as Spud turned to enter the store. As he strode to the door, a middle-aged man walked out and held out his hand, "Howdy, sir, my name's George Stockton. Is this your wagon? I saw it earlier when it was over by the livery. I never seen one with axles and wheels like that."

"Yeah, she's mine. Got her from a fellow that had it made in San An'tone. They got a new-fangled contraption there called a forge. They burn real hot and make what's called steel and the whole bed, axle and wheels are as strong as a train locomotive. My Pa does that back in Ohio. You never have to worry about changing a broken wheel or a busted axle with this one. You have to keep it greased like it was a machine or something but it sure is strong."

"I can see. You don't have much of a load for her and even less than this morning. Bet she could haul a lot."

"Yeah, lot more wagon than I needed, but I needed something at the time and you can't get too much of a good thing. Hate all the grease but she's been ready to go since I got her."

"Looks like a stock-man's outfit in there. You fixin' to haul your ridin' gear all over the country in the bed of a wagon?"

"Yeah, maybe. Really don't know what I'll do. My rear end is sick of sitting on a board all day. I was thinkin' of going on into Cheyenne and selling her and the horses and buy a saddle horse for the trip back. Be good to sit a saddle for a change."

"What's with those horses? Never seen anything as big and strong looking as that pair. I got a couple of draft horses that I thought was humdingers but not like those two."

"Them's called Percherons. They're French. They was bred to be draft animals over in Europe. Fellow had brought them in from New Orleans. Fellow what had the wagon was parting with them too. Bank had to take his place and he was moving into town. Didn't need either any more. Gave me a good deal on both."

"Percherons, uh? The ones I got are smaller and they're called Clydesdales. What a team it would make to put your pair as the wheel pair and mine as leads. They could pull a barn between them. What if you could find a buyer here? Any objections to selling now?"

"No, do you want the rig?"

"I'll tell you what I'm doin' right up front. I've been planning to start hauling in my own stock from St. Joe. The Cheyenne or Denver market just makes me pay someone else for doing what I could do. A couple a' teamsters and another wagon and my profit on each sale should pay about tenfold on my investment. Yours' looks like a trail buster and a half. What say we make a deal on them and you can put a horse under yourself right now?"

"I got nothing against that. What do you figure they're worth?"

"Would you part with the entire rig for twelve hundred?"

"Are you kidding? I'd part with my mother for that."

"Well I'm willing to pay. Saves me the trip to look for something that will, like as not, turn out to be nowhere near as good as yours. We'll just have to go to the bank for your money and you'll need to write out a bill of sale and we'll have it done. What were you doing when I jumped you?"

With a laugh, "I was going to give you some business. Need to pick up some supplies. Why don't we get this done now? I'll get my stuff finished after and be on my way. I have the bill of sale from the feller I got them from right here. I'll sign it over to you, take your money and we can both be about our business."

"Absolutely! Why don't you put the wagon behind my store and the horses in the barn around there? The bank is that building on the corner there. I'll meet you there as soon as I get my wife to mind the store."

Spud couldn't help thinking as he walked across the road toward the bank that this was just too easy. He liked doing business with the personable storekeeper. Haggling was not pleasant work, even if you had to do it to get by. Besides he had made more money on that stupid wagon than he would have made with a whole year pushing cows.

With the money that Skinny had given him and what he had saved for himself, a small place was well within his reach. Things were looking up, at least as well as they could without Skinny. He'd have to do it alone. There wouldn't be a pard on his new place, but if he was smart and worked he'd make it. He'd just have to make the best of it.

Spud strode into the bank. A businessman lookin' chap and the storekeeper were watching from a side office and Spud drug his spurs toward them and held out his hand toward the florid man in the business suit.

"Howdy, my name is Spud Turner."

"How do, young man. I'm Cyrus Vance and we're ready for you. If you could give me the bill of sale and have a seat I'll have the clerk bring out your money and we just need to sign some papers."

Pushing some papers toward Spud, "What are your plans now, sir?"

"Oh, get myself mounted and find work for the winter. Next spring, I'll be looking for a small place in Texas. I'm going to try to find one that I think I can make a go of. After that, I figure I'll be working too hard to have any plans at all."

"I'm impressed. Most men your age would be headed for a woman and drink. Maybe I can help. A mount could be a problem. The outlying ranches would be your best bet. They're putting up their mounts for the winter; they'll be green but a good deal and good animals. Here in town you're stuck with the livery stable. Make sure you're using your real name when you sign that. Spud is probably a nickname.

Anyway, the stable might be a problem. Gent that runs the place can be difficult and I don't know of anyone here in town that would sell a mount. Everyone's down to not needing to carry extra. Gets so you don't even need an animal here in town. A job is also hard. The only thing I know of as a possibility is the Rafter W. They had a man hurt. Could be they might need to replace him until he's back on his feet. I'm sure Sam Wilson will carry him until he's well but he might need someone to do his work until then.

I know all that's bad news but we finally get to your buy'n a place and there I'm your man. I can put you into a place like you've never seen in Texas. The grass here is the equal of any place on earth, and the land will grow anything if you give it water. Not to mention that the markets we're seeing in Chicago are just something for Texans to dream of."

Spud wasn't sure that you spelled Thomas that way, been way too long since he had tried. "Well I guess I'll tackle the horse and go from there. This is the second time I've heard of the Rafter W. Might be interesting to see what cowboyin' is like outside of Texas for a change. Is that a good place to work?"

"Best people that I know. Got a good cook. What else do you need?"

"'Bout all. How would a fellow get there?"

"Go down to the Cheyenne road and head west. After you cross the river, in about three miles you'll see a wagon road heading south to the old Wilkins place. About three miles farther on will be a wagon-track road bearing off toward the northwest. It's about two miles down that to the house. Tell Sam you talked to me and I sent you. Now, what are you going to do with all that money while you're working out there?"

"Watch it like a hawk on a mouse, I guess. Why do you ask?"

"Just thinkin' you might want to put it into the bank."

"I don't know. I always figured it could get stolen from the bank just like it could be stolen from me. Except if they took it from me they'd have to kill me and then I wouldn't care."

"Seems like sound reasoning to me, but we take precautions that you can't take. They'd have to get it out of the vault and that's not easy. They'd have to get out of town and that's not easy.

Then, your money wouldn't even be in the bank at all. We only have a small percentage of the money that people have deposited in the bank at one time. So they could only get a small part of your money anyway."

"What's a percentage?"

"Oh! Sorry! I mean just part of the money."

"Well, what if I wanted my money back?"

"In case you want your money is exactly why we have any money here at all. We keep just enough to give some people back their money if they want it. The rest we actually loan out for a profit. We would only have trouble if everyone wanted their money back at the same time. It would take maybe a week to get everyone's money back to them."

` "How can you give it to them if you loaned it out to someone else?"

With a hearty laugh, "Young man if you ever want to quit the cattle business and work in a bank just let me know. I'll find you a position somewhere. Well, what we would do is sell our outstanding loans to the Central Bank in Denver and they would send us the money to give back to our depositors. So, you see, the idea that you can lose your money when a bank gets robbed is just wrong. The only way to lose your money if it's in a bank is if the bank fails. That is, if the bank made loans that would not be repaid and I can assure you that that will never happen while I approve loans at this bank."

"So, if I wanted to take off for Texas I could get my money any time."

"Absolutely. However, I wouldn't advise you to do it that way if you were to ask my advice. You could just take enough for traveling expenses and write me to transfer the rest when you know where you'll be. I could pick out a good bank in the area and you would have your money in about a week. That way if someone tried to rob you on the trail, you wouldn't have to be killed to save it. I'd have it right here waiting for you."

"Dang! What's going to happen next? What a world we live in! There's no way I can come up short is there? I just give you my money and you take care of it for me."

"That's not even the best part. Let's say you want to spend some money at George's. You don't even need to give him any money. He has a bill that you can sign and I take the money out of your account and put it into his. Everybody gets what's owed, but I'm the only one who does anything. If you go to work for Sam, he can have your wages put into your account from his and you never see the money. What do you think of that?"

"Hang on to my twelve hundred and I'll be right back."

After a short time Spud was back at the counter pulling an oilcloth from under his shirt. He spread it out on the counter to reveal a stack of bills. "We might as well put it all in. It'll be good not to worry about it for a change."

The banker showed a little florid. "Mr. Turner, I think that that makes you about our largest depositor, which would make you eligible for a loan or anything else the bank can do for you. Also rest assured that no one but you and I will ever know that you have any money in the bank much less how much.

I swear I get so used to dealing with people that are just plain ordinary. I had forgotten what a truly exceptional person was like. You, sir, are very definitely exceptional. Please if you do stay around here, consider making it permanent. We need young men like you and you can depend on me to make it as easy for you as I can, any time I can." With an extended hand, "Good luck to you"

"Thank you sir. I'll sure give it some thought."

Chapter Five

He wormed around to ease a lump under him and snuggled down into the warm blankets. The steam from his breath showed him that winter wasn't far off in this northern country. He should have been up an hour ago and on his way by now but throwing back his covers and getting out in the cold was more than he was prepared to do just yet. That was his reward to himself for a job well done.

At last his eyes opened and he looked around. The first thing Spud settled on was the horse he had bought in town. If anyone could show me an uglier jug head, I'd fork over ten bucks to'im. That damn hostler had several mounts that would have been fine but that one was all he would sell and at an unreasonable price at that.

Oh well, he could either shoot him or make a pack animal out of him when he got to a ranch and could get mounted.

Spud jerked bolt upright, all laziness gone. You could trust an animal to let you know what was around and that ugly excuse for a jackass was about to sound off to his cousins somewhere. Spud was beside him in three springs. The horse was startled and tried to shy away but his picket held. Spud placed his hand over his nostrils, rubbing gently. Better to know what's around before it found out about you than vice-versa was a wisdom that had been pounded into him practically from birth.

With the horse under control, Spud considered his position. Over the years, the spring flooding of the creek had carved out an open expanse on the north bank. Spud had chosen here because of the protection the step southern bank afforded him. He pulled the pin and led the horse farther back into the "v" shape of the cut bank and reset his picket line.

Watching the animal to prevent his sounding off, Spud picked up his rifle from beside his hastily abandoned bedroll. He tossed his tarp, slicker and blanket toward his ditty bag and surveyed the north bank, ready for a fast retreat if necessary.

On the south side, the creek flowed right up against maybe a ten-foot bank. For sure you weren't going to see anything until it topped that bank. Before he could do anymore figuring, a sound off to the south told him what he needed to know. Watching the horse all the time he worked his way to the top of the south bank until he could peep over the top.

About a' half mile up the creek was what had caused the entire ruckus. There were five horsemen working their way down to the creek in order to ford and go on up in the direction that the road took. Why they were off the road by a mile was the first thought that occurred to Spud, but a lot of people were cautious these days, and the road had highwaymen you could be sure. They were a suspicious looking lot, dingy and unkempt. Spud watched the lead mount.

The visage painted was that of a bear mounted on the nicest moving black he'd ever seen. Spud stared with envy as the magnificent beauty pranced down to the creek, forded and like a cat moved out of sight on the other side. The other four mounted men and two pack animals followed him out of sight. Spud slid back to his hastily abandoned campsite, "Yeah, just look at you! Aren't you ashamed of yourself? Looking like you do in the same neighborhood as something that looks as good as that beauty. Well, you should be! Come on; let's get ready to go! Better not build a fire with them around.

By the time we get packed they'll be gone and we can get on over to the W and see if we're here or on to Texas. At least we can get you a companion. One that can carry me for several days in a row, that'll relegate you to carryin' a pack."

You could see the buildings over the prairie for a long way. They rose up from a sea of waving grass as high as his horse's belly. As Spud drew nearer, he saw what looked like a well-run ranch start to sprout up. You could see the barn, two sheds and the corral before the house was visible. Spud knew first-hand how much work went into keeping them in the good shape they were in. At his last place of employment, he had kept up the Lazy J almost by himself. Well maybe with a little help, and, he had to admit, this layout looked even better than the J.

Pulling up before what must have been the bunkhouse but was actually attached to the ranch house, Spud sat his horse and watched a fellow make his way to him.

"Step down there stranger. My name is Sam Wilson. What can I do for you?"

Spud looked at a tall, slim, white-headed man with the browned skin of an outdoors person as he stepped down from his mount. "Howdy, Mr. Wilson. My name's Spud Turner and talk in town was that you might need some help and was hiring. Rode out to see if you might put me on for the winter."

"No, sorry young fellow. 'Fraid they were mistaken in town. Got all the help I need right now. Hate to see you come all this way for nothing, but I can't use you."

"Sorry to hear that sir. Everyone says you're real good to work for but if you're not hiring, you're not hiring. Guess I'll be on my way and thank you."

"Yeah, sure sorry, but no need to run off. We'll have lunch ready soon. Why don't you wait and have a meal with us. Least I can do after you rode all this way to check on a job."

"Well, thank you. Sure am hungry (thinking of the missed breakfast). Think I might take you up on that."

"Well, fine Mr. Turner. You can put your animal in the corral and wash up in the bunkhouse over there. If you like you can put up here for the night and get a good start in the morning. Just tell the boys I said you were welcome."

"Well, thank you Mr. Wilson."

Walking into the bunkhouse, Spud saw three men lounging there. There was one in the bunk, probably the injured man, one sitting at a plank table with benches and one propped back in a chair in the back. "Howdy, boys. Mr. Wilson said to hang out here 'til lunch. Hope tha's all right?"

"Have to be. He's the boss. But, it would be just fine even if he wasn't. Nobody goes hungry here. Why don't you throw your stuff on that bunk over there and sit down here," said the man at the table, pointing to the opposite side from where he was.

Spud looked at a middle-aged to older man who had his hat pulled low and was working on a bridle. "Thanks. My name's Spud."

"Howdy, mine's Blacky. That cripple in the bunk's Pete and the long one in the back is Stick."

"Nice to meet you boys." Sinking down onto the bench that faced the back of the large open room.

A couple of "Howdys" came out. "Where you from Spud?" The man across the table inquired.

"Came up from Texas way."

"Yeah, thought I heard Texas in your voice. Fixin' to stay long?"

"No. Just lunch and head on out."

"Well what brought you by?"

"Looking for work, but your boss isn't hiring. Guess I'll head on back to Texas now."

"Just tell me to shut up if I'm getting too nosy, but you came up here from Texas to ask for a job and now your headed back there?"

"I don't mind. No, I had a chore to do and now that it's finished, I'm going home."

"You're harder to get anythin' out of than a clam. Way you say it this chore must be some deep, dark secret."

With a laugh, "No, I just didn't know if you wanted me to talk your ear off. Sometimes people don't want to spend all their time listenin' to some galoot talk about himself."

"You make them ask a direct inquiry just to be sure they's really interested uh?"

With another laugh, "That's about it. Don't want to put myself off on anyone. What I was doing was bring my pard up here to plant him. He died about a month ago and asked me to bury him here."

Blacky kept the straightest face in the county as he said, "Now see. I knew you had something interesting to say. Not like the yahoos I have to associate with around here. You should just listen to the crap what these boring gents have to say, if you can get them to talk at all. Was this home for your departed friend?"

"Yeah, he was born here and he was raised on his folks place around here somewhere."

"Been here longer than anyone 'cept the Indians, what's his name. Might be I know'd him."

"His name was Skinny Warren."

"You buried ol' Skinny?"

"I did. You know him?"

"Know him? Why he worked here when he was just a shaver. He was here when I hired on. We was like brothers for too many years to count. You buried him uh? What happened?"

"It was a horse. We brought some stock in to green break and then turn them loose for the winter. Planning to bring them back in and finish them for roundup next spring. He didn't make it."

"No! You're not telling me that some green nag did in Skinny Warren. That's hard to believe! Why, he hardly ever even got throwed! Wasn't a horse in a hundred that could put him off much less hurt him bad."

"I know. Sure enjoyed puttin' down the jug head that did the deed. Damned nag wasn't anything special. We put Skinny on her and when we gave'r her head, dammed if she didn't run full blast into the corral fence. One of the busted rails popped up and stuck Skinny in the belly and he went flyin' off and stuck it even deeper when he landed. He lived almost a week but the doc said there was no hope. Skinny made me promise to bring him here and told me where to put him. And I just got it done now."

"Sure sorry, youngster! World won't be as good a place without Skinny in it. That's for sure. You must have been close to do all that for him."

"Yeah, I owed him a lot more than that. He practically raised me. Taught me about all I know about cows, that's for sure."

A gruff voice from the back spoke up, "Whyn't you just bury him down there? It's not like he would ever know. Him bein' dead and all."

Spuds eyes rose from the table and surveyed the longest man he had ever seen. Maybe he had seen taller men but not taller and skinnier, and this one had a head of hair the color of a tomato it was so red. This man would tower above everyone and wasn't bigger around that a fence post.

"I guess the answer to that is that I would have known even if Skinny wouldn't. I would have known that I didn't even care enough to keep my word. I don't think that would have set well in my stomach. Maybe that fits in yours but not mine."

The long man stood up. "You say'n I aint as good as you? Is that what you're sayin'?"

Spud without hurrying stood. Only the man in the bunk was able to say how the gun got in his hand, but it was cocked and hanging loosely in his grasp by the time he became fully erect.

"I ain't sayn' anything. Just responding to what you said. Where I'm from we draw meaning from a man's words and it sounds like you said that to me."

"Where do you get off coming in here and pulling a gun on me?"
You could see he was measuring his chances and did not like them.
"Ain't no Texas saddle tramp can get away with that. Even it up and we'll see who's telling who."

"Don't see anything uneven about it. You goin' to back up your mouth or not?"

As if on cue, the door to the bunkhouse swung open and a giant filled it up. This guy was so big that his head looked like it belonged to someone else who would have been considerly smaller. His shoulders and chest were so far around they made his head look like it would better fit on a doll.

Spud's eyes never wavered from the tall, skinny cowboy in front of him. "What the hell is going on here?" the big man in the door exclaimed.

Silence was his answer.

"Somebody better start explaining this", he demanded. "Blackie, what the hell is happening?"

"Don't look at me June, I ain't in this. It's these two rannies here that's squared off on each other."

"Would someone like to tell me how this got started and now would be a good time?"

The voice from the bunk said, "The stranger was telling a story when Stick said more than he should have and the stranger called him."

"Dammit, Stick! Is that true?"

Silence answered him. "Stick, I swear to God I'm going to plug you myself if you don't start answerin' me."

"I don't know who you are, but maybe I could help you." Spud offered to the big man without moving his eyes.

"Cowboy, make no mistake I'm your maker. Now you need to put that hog leg up and let's get to the bottom of this."

"Don't see how I can do that. This skinny drink of water might shoot me."

The giant growled, "From this moment on, the only person in this room that gets shot will be shot by me. Stick, you sit down! Stranger you put up that pistol and sit down. I'll get this straightened out. Stick, dammit, sit down now! Stranger, you need to back up just a little and give everyone some room!"

As Stick slouched into his chair, Spud said," I don't know if that would be a good idea with the way you're talking."

"Cowboy you really don't have any choice. I'll drop you where you stand and with the way you're facing it'll be easy enough to do. Just put it up and I promise you that I'll at least sort this out to my satisfaction and that's been good enough for twenty years on this place."

"Good point," Spud said as he slid his colt home and continued standing.

The big man noted his standing and decided it wasn't over just yet, "Stick, you work here so you get first crack. What's going on here?"

"Aw, June, this galoot comes in here acting all important and makin' all kinds 'a claims. I just asked him what was what and out comes his gun."

Pete, is that it?"

"No, June. Not in my book. Kid was just talkin' to Blackie when Stick jumps in an' starts challenging him. Stranger wouldn't take it and that's when you showed up just in the nick of time, I'll say. I thought ol' Stick had bought the farm this time."

"Stick, you heard it. Is Pete lying?"

Silence.

"Stick!" The voice was so low and menacing that it made the hair on your neck stand up. You knew if someone died at his hands today they wouldn't be the first.

"All right. Dammit, no he's not," Stick growled.

"Well, I said you get first talk, but that's a double edge. It cuts both ways because I also know you better than this gent. And this is it. I've put up with you not getting along with anyone for as long as I'm going to. I think that you could be a steady hand and a fellow to ride with, but you go and muck it up with always getting nasty.

I'm through! I tell you what's going to happen. You're to get up now and head out to the Willows outrider shack. You don't want to do that, then you just keep on ridin' off this spread!

If you go to the line shack, tell George he's to come on in here and work 'til spring. You stay up there for the winter. That should give you plenty of time to think and this is what I want you to think about.

You decide if you can come back here and get along with everyone. And I mean everyone! You decide what's wrong with you that you can't get along and you fix it. If you show back up down here next spring I expect you to be the easiest fellow in the world to get along with or I expect you to find work on someone else's spread. Do you understand that?"

"Yes."

"Good.   Then git!"

Everyone watched in silence as Stick made a show of slamming items into his blankets and, rolling them up, stomping to the door and out.

The big man watched him leave and turned toward Spud, "My name's June Frocker and I run this place."

"Mine's Spud Turner. Met Mr. Wilson. Didn't know about you."

"Well now you do. Not intendin' to be hostile or nothin', but nothing happens here without me sayin' it does. You don't fight nobody or shoot nobody without my say-so. Can you live with that?"

"Guess I can live with anything and have. For myself I got an invite to lunch and accepted with every intention of leaving out when it was over. If nobody wants to brace me between now and then we should be fine."

"Sounds like a workin' proposition to me, Spud. Welcome to the Rafter W. The best spread this side of hell."

"Well thank ya' kindly, Segundo. I hear you got a good cook too."

"You got that right. Although it takes him forever to get it ready. Blackie what're you doing here. Lazin' around waitin' for lunch. Don't you have anything to do?"

"Doin' somethin' now! As for what I'm going to do- got to take that pump into town and might's well wait 'til I et before I go in. Don't you think?"

"Yeah, sure. Where you from Spud?" As he lowered his bulk onto the bench opposite Spud. The bench groaned loudly.

"Texas."

"Spud buried Skinny Warren!"

"What?" The big man with the little head paused. "Guess he was dead when you did that?"

"Yep! Died about a month ago. Put him in your cemetery yesterday."

"He said some loco bronc put a corral rail through his chest."

There was a long silence before the big man raised his tiny head to look at Spud. "Your putting him in the ground says that you two were close. Had you known him long?'

"Yeah. Since I hit Texas, 'bout seven years now. He sort of took me under his wings and schooled me on about ever' thing. Best pard a man could have!"

"I see. Guess you don't know that he was part of this place a while back?"

"I told 'im. Just afore you came in."

"Yeah, gave him a job when his folks died. Sam bought out his spread; it's part of this place now. He turned into the best hand I ever had after I had schooled him some. Never thought I'd go before him. Sure leaves a hollow feeling inside to hear it."

"Ain't that a hoot? Here you taught him, then he taught me and now I'm sitting across the table from you. Ain't this old world a strange place sometime?"

"Recon so! Well I got work to do before lunch. See you guys later." The floor protested with every step as he made his way out.

They sat and talked for a time. "Come on Spud, we wash up this way."

After both of them helped Pete from the bunk, Spud followed the older man out a side door into a long runway that was screened in and had a pump and washbasin set up on a long bench.

"Wow, this is nice! Who thought of this?"

"The old man had us build this maybe eight, ten years ago. We got some sides in the barn that we put up over the screens in the winter. You can go between what used to be the old bunkhouse and the new bunkhouse without even getting cold or wet. We like it, you bet!"

They led Spud through the other end of the runway into a large room with a long table and chairs situated in the middle of what was obviously the dining room, but had at one time been the bunkhouse.

The group waited on Pete to get seated. A guy Spud had not seen before put Pete's crutches away, and everybody got situated. The big foreman sat at the far head of the table and Spud waited for the others to seat themselves in case they always sat in the same spot. He chose a seat next to Blackie and watched as Mr. Wilson walked in and stood at the head of the table facing June.

"We have a visitor for this meal. For those who haven't met him yet this is Spud Turner, late of Texas." Seating himself, "Also, some of you know or have heard of Skinny Warren, a gent who has friends in these parts. Our guest apparently buried him yesterday and we should pay respects to the memory of our departed comrade. If we could all bow our heads for a few moments of silence at his passing, I would appreciate it."

Spud admired the way Mr. Wilson talked and spent the time watching the others at the table. There were two that Spud had not met. They were a little older than Spud and had given him a friendly nod when they came in. At Mr. Wilson's nod, there was a lot of commotion until their plates were heaping.

"Mr. Turner, it seems that I owe you an apology."

With a startled look on his face Spud said, "What in thunder for!"

"Well as June is want to do, it has been pointed out to me that I made judgments about you without botherin' to get to know you. I'm afraid that I judged you to be a saddle tramp when I saw you this morning and now I have to eat that judgment. I'm sorry, young fellow. Hope you don't hold any hard feelings."

"Oh, Mr. Wilson, there's lots of folks who've gotten to know me real well and still came to that conclusion. So I don't know how I could feel badly toward you. Think nothing of it."

"One thing is still botherin' me young man! Where in hell did you get that ugly mount of yours and why?"

With a chuckle, "You got me where I'm embarrassed at all right. Kind of hate to be seen riding him but that's all I could find to buy in town. Sold my wagon and hitch in town and sure needed something. Afraid he's the only thing that I could find to buy. Was hopin' you could let me buy a good mount when I got here."

"You get him from the livery?"

"Yeah. He was all the owner would sell, so I was stuck with him."

"Um. Johnson came in from the Black Hills couple a' years ago and bought that place from the feller that owns the saloon. Folks around here think he brought his morals with him from the gold fields. Not like what we want around here. Might be time he learned that we deal with people like we'll have to see them again tomorrow.

Tell you what young man, June wants to give you a job if you still want it and I've withdrawn any objections I had. If you want to take a job with us at least until spring, I'll take that swayback off your hands. You can pick three from the ramada for your use and keep the one you like as the replacement for this mount if you decide to leave us next spring. How's that?"

"Well, sir, I think that I would like it here for the winter, but you've got no reason to help me out with the horse. I maybe can use him for a pack animal next spring. I don't know, but I can't shuffle him off on you. Wouldn't be fair!"

"Well, then you're hired. Welcome to the Rafter W. As for the horse, you're not shufflin' him off. I'm goin' to take him back to Johnson and get your money back for him. What did the old skinflint charge you?"

"Don't know that's fair either. We shook hands on the deal even if he did have me over a barrel."

"Maybe you don't understand young man, but this is a community. We're all in this together and Johnson needs to understand that. There's been talk with him before. He knows that to continue as a part of our community he needs to act better. Looks like he saw you as an outsider and fleeced you. I'm just goin' to show him the light."

"I see! Kind of between him and the neighbors, uh? Well, all right. I gave him sixty-five dollars for the horse and I want all to know that I argued for over an hour a'for I forked that over. Hope you have better luck with him than I did."

"Not a matter of luck. He takes him back or learns to have his bowl movements around that jug head's carcass. I really don't care which. Fleecing people does not go here and everyone in town will tell him the same thing."

They finished their meal in silence and with great gusto.

June said, "Blackie, why don't you hold off on town until we can get Spud situated. Maybe he'll need to ride in with you for some outfit. If we can't get his mounts settled in time you might need to wait until tomorrow to go in. Show Spud where to get the hackamores and I'll meet both of you down at the ramada.

Everyone rose and moved out of the house. "You can get three halters from that shed over there. I'll saddle a horse and meet you down that way."

"Right"

The big guy was standing beside a saddled mule gazing at a loosely bunched group of horses. Spud offered, "Hey, June. How green are these?"

"We'll have fun this afternoon. That's why I kept Blackie. They shouldn't be too bad, they were all ridden last month, but you'll get some exercise."

Spud could feel the big foreman's eyes on him as he judged the animals. "If you like to get others opinions, I sure like that dappled gray to the left there. She really impresses me with the way she moves and she's really built compact."

"How'd you know I was looking at her? You're right! She's beautiful! I'll put money she can fly. Look at the way she holds her head."

"Yeah!"

"Blacky rode up and started to dismount. Spud asked, "Why in the world is she still here. Someone must have passed over her before."

"Everybody passed on her. You know how cowboys are; they think they'll be roping all day long. That's what they like and they want a big stud to lay them flat. Nobody ever thinks that they spend three weeks a year branding and the rest of the year herding. That little gray will make the best cutting horse in the territory or I miss my guess."

Blackie piped up, "You giving the youngster the benefit of your vast knowledge?"

"I think he's right. She's the best in this lot. How come you never took her, June?"

"I can't use a horse. They start having trouble with their knees and ankles if I try to work them. I'm just too big. That's my mule over there. That big jack can haul me all day. If we're working cattle, I have to do the work off a horse. I brand and throw them, things like that. She'll be fine ropin' if you don't ask her to do it all day. What else do you like?"

"That big roan is put together and that sorrel will do. Let's get them."

June and Blackie rode in and dropped a loop on the three identified and Spud put a halter on each in its turn. Leading them to the corral, Spud had them ridden in short order with the others saddling each for him.

"That sure didn't take long. You guys think that you'll have time to get into town today?"

Blackie spoke up. "No, might just as well wait til first thing in the morning."

"Ok! Spud I was thinking you might go along with him. Mainly, you need to get some winter clothing. I took a peek at your knap sack and I think you'll need a heavier coat, some long johns and socks. Blackie can tell you what's best and give you some good advice about making it through the winter.

You're going to have to pay close attention to the weather. I know it gets cold in Texas, but not like here. You'll see twenty below for sure and maybe forty or fifty if it's a bad winter. We'll lose stock if it gets that cold. Make sure you're in the line camp until she blows over (Maybe two three days- sometime a week). Then you'll need to get out and save all that needs it.

Most important, don't get caught out when it starts. Get into that cabin with plenty of firewood already cut. If you do get caught out, take the bridle off your mount (the bit will freeze in its mouth) and let it go. Dig into the leeward side of a snowdrift, keeping the entrance as small as you can. Once you get back in, dig a dome out above you. That'll hold the heat from you and keep you warm. It's called a snow cave and you'll be fine until she blows out."

June picked up a stick. "The ranch is here. That's the Platte and we have creeks here, here and here. The road back to town runs this way and there are some mountains here and here. You'll find a creek here and the line cabin is on the west bank. You can't miss it once you're on the creek.

You can get grub from the back of the kitchen and more when you need it. Get a packsaddle from that shed and I'll see you when I get up that way. Ask Blackie about anything you didn't understand." Extending his hand, they shook and then June walked away.

Chapter Six

Blacky and Spud had made two of the chosen horses into pack animals. They were loaded and tied to the wagon. The gray was saddled but tied also. Blacky, clucking at his team, decided that now was the time to educate the new man to Nebraska Territory.

"The biggest danger to the stock is definitely the weather. You'll just need to keep them pushed down from the hills into the level valley where they can find grass while the weather's good. Once it starts to get cold, you'll need to be smart, about yourself and the animals. Even up here, the animals will make it if they don't fall and you keep the ice busted up over the ponds so they can get water. I'll bet it's not much different from Texas 'cept up here you can die.

The worst thing is the wind. It'll just plain kill you. If you get wet and you're in the wind, you only got maybe ten minutes to live in the open. A smart man would make two-three places to shelter if you can't make it back to the cabin. That snow cave idea June told you about will work.

Plenty of fellows have made it through some bad ones that way, but you have to wait until the snow gets deep enough to build one. Thing you have to be sure of is make your entrance on the lee side and make it small. Then you need to get a good dome inside. That last one's what most people don't savvy. Do you see how it works?"

"Sure, you dome it so the heat rising from your body gets trapped up in the dome and heats up the place."

"That's right; you Texicans ain't as bad as I heard. You also want to keep a saddle gun on you."

"Injun trouble?"

"Naw! We don't have no problems with them. We got Pawnee up here and they's downright reasonable. Ain't never had no trouble from them and they're so tough not many raids from other tribes come down here.

You don't need to worry about them; you see some just act friendly and helpful. You're going to be surprised about them.

You got 'Pache down there. Hear they's trouble! The Pawnee are a handsome and noble people. The Ol' Man even married one. Been several years since she passed on, but she was one of the prettiest ladies in the whole territory. You need the gun, at least until about December for bears."

"Never had any trouble with bears before. Why here?"

"You don't have Grizzly in Texas."

"Oh, yeah, heard some about them. What's so dangerous about 'em?"

"You know about that part of the Bible that says you're walkin' in the valley and not bein' afraid? Well, that's the Grizzly. Only he's not afraid 'cause he's the baddest son-of-a-bitch in the valley.

Wait 'til you see a Grizz' walk along. You can see he's never seen anything he can't whip. Looks like a king, the way they move. Now most times they just goin' to lord it over you and go on, but with them you never know. They might take it in their mind that day to kill everything they see, and you better be ready.

Just let 'em go if they will. Ever' once in a while they'll kill a beef but not often and the old man says to just let 'um have that. Worst thing in the world is one that's woke up from his siesta. You see a grizz in January; just kill it outright, 'cause he's goin' to kill you if you don't.

"Then there's the big cats. Cougs'll be up where you are and the ol' man says just kill them. Wolves too. You'll see animals that need doctorin' from a' attack and you'll find wounded critters that got hurt by an attack. You had them in Texas, uh?"

"Sure, we killed them too. Lost too much young stock to them. Been my experience they're hard to find. Used to have men with dogs come in and run them to ground. Cleared them out that way."

"Yeah, tell Sam. Maybe we could bring in some hounds from back east and do a deed on the varmints."

"I will. Or, you tell him. Might be a time before I see him. I guess a storm here is just like a storm in Texas. It starts getting dull and cloudy, you know something's goin' to happen."

"Yeah, this's not magic land. It's just you got to take it serious here. In Texas you might get as cold as ten below but here, at its worst, it might be twenty to forty below. Don't wait to see what it's like before you act. You see it coming, head for the line shack then. If you find out you ain't going to make it, get to the safe place you set up already. Another thing, get the bit off your horse. Metal'll freeze to his mouth if you don't."

They had made it to the main road and were headed east by this time. Spud asked, "Do we cut off to the south to get to the line shack from the road?"

"Yeah, maybe two miles farther. We'll picket the pack animals there and go on into town without them. You can pick them up on the way back"

"Yeah, sure."

Breaking the silence, Blacky offered, "You know, Spud, ever since you came up with Skinny dyin, I been thinkin' about them days. Skinny took off to see what was over the hill and I just stayed put. We's just the same, two young squirts with no brains, but he went all over and I just been here all this time."

Spud picked up on what Blackie meant right away. "I see your point, but when it came time to light, Skinny came back here. Also, I been watchin' you for two days and you seem to be happy here. The people you've known and worked with for so long care about you. All in all, seems like it really didn't make any difference.

What everyone's looking for from others is right inside them all the time. No matter what you and Skinny decided to do, folks just wound up liking both of you. It's more what you had inside that counted, don't you think?"

"Kid, you sound like one o' them phi-los-o-phers. I can see why Skinny stuck with you. You know that June thought of him as his kid. He gave you a job 'cause you was Skinny's friend."

"I saw. When he said that about 'goin' first' I knew he thought of him as special. Course he was. Wasn't anyone who didn't love Skinny."

They rode in silence to the picket-point. Spud put the pack animals out and they resumed their way toward town. Blackie again broke the silence. "You got a girl waitin' for you back home, Spud?"

"Sure do! Got the prettiest gal in

two counties said she'd wait for me."

"You gonna' marry her?"

"We got a understandin' of sorts. Her Pa' says I'll have to get settled first. He don't want his daughter to marry a cowboy."

"Smart feller! You don't sound too sure, though!"

"That's not it, I'm sure. She's all a man could want, and I'm sure lucky to get her. It's just that she's like some heifer that placidly follows the lead bull around. Even if she knows a better path, she still just follows. I don't know- maybe she's just young. And her Pa's real pushy."

Blackie pulled up in front of the general store just in time to see Mr. Wilson coming out to meet them.

"Howdy Sam. You was off and gone awful early this morning. Did you figure to enjoy your work?"

""Howdy boys, you up to no good? Hey, Blackie, Yeah, thought I might enjoy today's chore. That the pump you got in back?"

"Yep, did you see the hostler yet?"

"Sure 'nuff. Got Spud's money and set ever' thing right." Reaching into his pocket. "Here Spud. I figure this twenty was overpaid for my horse, so you get it back. What brought you to town?"

"Forty five's all you want for that gray? That's the one I figure to keep."

"She looks good and solid." Running an appreciative eye over the horse tied to the back of the wagon

"June thought I had better get some clothes for cold weather. Said you could never be sure about when the first storm would come in."

"Can't argue with him there. George just got in some new sheepskin coats that I've been eyein'. Take a look at them. Is Blacky supposed to give you advice on what to get?"

"Sure am. Aim to make a real Beau Brummel out of him. Hey Boss the kid's got some ideas about how to get rid of the cougars. Says they brought in gents with dogs that would run them down."

"Well, sounds like it would work. I'll look into it. Spud I'll leave you in good hands. I'll get on back. If you need to put any or all on the ranch account, just do it. I'll take it out of your salary. Tell Stockton I said it was ok."

"Thanks Mr. Wilson, but that's not necessary. I'll just pay for them and get on out to the line shack. See you next spring."

"Sure but I'll be around before then. I try to stop by a couple of times. Maybe bring you something fresh to eat. How do you like pies?"

"I'd sell my soul for a cherry pie."

"Is that right. Well, no promises but I'll see what I can do."

Chapter Seven

It was getting dark by the time Spud made it back to the picketed packhorses. They had not been molested and were grazing peacefully with their packs still secure. Picking them up and getting strung out on a well-worn path beside the small creek took no time at all, but Spud knew that full dark would overtake him before he reached the cabin. That was ok. He could fumble around in the dark as well as anybody.

There would be lanterns and he could always get things straight in the morning. He and Blacky had eaten in town so all he needed to do was get the horses taken care of and a bed for himself. Blackie had said to keep on the west side and he would run right into the cabin.

The sound of his horse's hoofs and sway of the saddle had beaten a rhythm into Spud's head and made him drowsy as the trail skirted a grove of trees and dipped close to the creek bank. When he cleared the trees, the cabin came unexpectedly into view. There was a light.

What in the world? There shouldn't be any light. Why was someone there? The young man pulled up and sat his horse. Maybe another of the ranch hands had come out from the ranch while he had been in town. Maybe someone had brought him a message. None of this made good sense and Spud made a decision.

There wasn't much room, but he got his cavalcade turned and after backtracking around the grove of trees, he cut off the trail that had narrowed coming from the other direction. He led the animals deep into the wooded area and dismounted. Securing all three, Spud squatted in the dark to think. If he were to sneak up on a legitimate comrade there would be some hazing, but if he rode into a hornets nest he could be killed.

The course was all too clear. Stepping to his saddlebags, Spud removed his boots and got an extra revolver and moccasins from them. Setting off under the cover of the forest, he made his way to the windowless west side of the cabin. He could hear some noise but not well enough to figure out what was going on. He had seen light coming from a window in the cabin on the side facing the creek and Spud made his way very carefully to this vantage point.

Now, the sound was much louder. There was obviously a fight going on. The unmistakable sound of fist hitting flesh was clearly audible. The skin stretched across the window had a crack between the hide and window casing in one corner and Spud carefully peeked into this.

Just in time to see some big guy hit a smaller man in the stomach. The little man went flying across the room to alight in a heap against the far wall. Except that brief glimpse of the flying body revealed it was not a man at all. That was a WOMAN!

What the hell! The boy sank down against the outside wall and pondered his predicament. There were four men in there and that one woman. The big man was going to kill the woman if he did not stop and he showed no sign of wanting to do that. On the other hand, four to one was not good. If he showed himself, there was a good chance that would be the last thing he ever did.

Sounds told the story of the women being hit again. Was there any way he was going to stay hidden and listen to that? No, not really! He knew he had to do something. If he was going to show himself at all best to go strong.

Maybe if he stepped into the door with both guns covering the men he could get them unarmed. If they all started shooting, he knew he couldn't get them all. From the looks of them, these were not gentle people.

Spud remembered that the lamp would go out if guns started going off in a close space. Remember to keep moving if anything happened, he told himself. He considered what could be expected to happen. Maybe this was the day! Well, good enough! No use to over think it. He made his way to the door and pushed it open.

Immediately stepping into the cabin, "Everyone just stand easy." There was the big guy apart from the other three standing in a knot at one end of the cabin, and the woman was crumpled on the floor. Spud pointed a gun at each group and moved farther into the room, pushing the door out of his way, "Ok boys. Nobody make any sudden moves or I'll kill you. What are you doing here?"

The startled men were frozen for a beat or two. If the boy had been a little older and more hardened he would have just started shooting, but experience hadn't taught him that it was better to live and kill than to die without blood on your hands.

Standing under the menace of two guns, the big man was the first to move. With surprising quickness for a big man, he took a step and swiped at the lamp. Spud shot him and moved just as the room was plunged into total darkness.

Spud moved against the east wall as bullets smacked into the wall behind where he had been previously. He picked out a gun flash, fired at it and moved again. He heard a grunt and clang as he bumped into someone. He put a bullet into whoever was there and moved again.

After the deafening sounds of multiple gunshots in a small room, the brief silence was awesome. Suddenly the door was flung open and a figure went flying out. Spud snapped a shot after the shadow and was about to shoot someone who was moving toward the door close behind the shadow. At the last instance, he held up. The figure fled through the door. No use to kill someone who was running away.

His every sense strained the dark. Since the door had opened the interior wasn't so black and Spud was pretty sure he was alone. Then he remembered the woman. She couldn't wait forever. No sound was made.

Watching the door, Spud took out a match and with his skin crawling, struck it. The flickering light showed him alone in the room with a motionless bundle piled against the back wall and the guy he had bumped into crumpled to the floor where Spud had shot him.

Quickly blowing out the match, Spud dropped to the floor and crawled to the door to peek out. Two horsemen were leaving the barn. They were bareback and carrying their saddles and bridles in their arms as they frantically beat a path out of there.

They burst across the open space and around the trees out of sight. One was hurt. Still watching out the door, Spud picked up the lantern. He closed the door and striking a new match lit the lantern.

First he repaired the slit on the window, then Spud bent over the prone shape. He was dead. The other figure proved to be also. Gently rolling the woman onto her back, he exposed the damage done to her face.

There were viscous gashes on her left cheekbone and her left eye was swollen shut, bleeding, and cut. The whole side of her face was already huge. Her mouth was split open and there was blood everywhere. The pulse was still strong in her throat and Spud decided that she needed repairs as job one.

Setting the lantern down, all the while lamenting the broken chimney because the light was feeble and guttering, Spud picked up the women and placed her gently on the table. His sewing kit was back on the animals and he would have to be careful.

Palming his gun he opened the door and quickly stepped outside and just as quickly moved away from it into the shadows of the cabin.

Pausing to probe the darkness, he could detect nothing. Spud quickly moved to his horses and led them into the barn. There were four horses already there and after removing the packs he turned his out into the corral. Promising to come back and take care of them later, he grabbed one pack and made for the door.

Since he was usually the only one sober on a Saturday night, Spud had plenty of practice fixing up the damage done by fist fighting. Besides showing him the futility of pounding on other humans, it had also made him very skilled in the art of repair.

He rummaged around in the kitchen part of the cabin and located a crock of vinegar on a shelf. Somebody had liked pickles and it would do as a disinfectant. Placing the lamp and the dead men's gun on a wall shelf, Spud put the vinegar beside the damaged women. Pulling from his pack a clean cloth and his sewing kit, he began his work.

After washing his hands, he set about closing the wounds on her face. She had already started to clot so Spud almost reverently wiped and soaked her face in the vinegar until he could see the gashes clearly. Retrieving his needle and thread from the vinegar, he started the arduous and time-consuming task of sewing up the wounds.

Satisfied that he could do no better a job, he decided to check her ribs.

Here was the danger. Taking the tick mattress from the bed, Spud made a pillow to prop her part way up on it, and unbuttoned the remaining buttons that hadn't been broken on her torn shirt. She sure enough was a women but she had some hideous bruises on her left side. That guy was a solid right-hander.

Wondering how in the hell he had missed shooting him from so close up, Spud gently pushed at the ribs and decided after close examination that they were surely broken, but that they did not seem to be protruding into her lungs. They all seemed to be in place.

He could wrap her up to hold them and get a doctor's opinion tomorrow. Finding the bandages in his pack he accomplished this, put one of his shirts on her, and laid her on the nearest bunk.

He listened for noise outside and deciding there was nothing wrong he pulled the dead men out to the back of the cabin and went to the horses. He shooed all three into the barn and under the light of a lamp, rubbed them dry with a gunnysack. Putting the three outlaws horses out into the corral, Spud put out grain for his three and trudged to the back of the cabin.

He stacked firewood on top of the bodies to keep animals from them and then went into the cabin. Taking a chair from the table he propped it against the wall beside the door and closed his eyes. It had been a long and arduous day.

∞

Spud jerked awake with a start. It was almost light. He had fallen asleep some time during the night, but everything seemed to be fine. He listened without moving for a while and decided all was as it should be. Stretching and moving around he decided to see what had happened to the two varmints who had fled.

Before leaving he checked the woman. She seemed to be sleeping better after making small noises for most of the night.

Grabbing his boots he took off the moccasins and put them on. Slipping out the door, he saddled the gray and followed the marks of the horses from the previous night. They traveled a short piece and one stopped. The other stopped a short distance away and milled unattended.

Then both took off to the west toward the Cheyenne Road. Spud followed to the road and rode a short piece along its southern border to see if they had cut off. Seeing nothing, he returned to the cabin.

Slipping into the cabin to check on his charge he found himself staring at the business end of the gun he had stashed on the shelf. The eyes that could barely see were not wavering at all. A muffled and barely audible voice asked, "Who are you? Stop moving!"

"Well, I see you're alive, if only barely."

"Yes, and if you want to go on in that condition, you'll start explaining."

"Well, ma'am it seems that I'm the only one here who doesn't need to explain. That gun may say differently, but you're the one who doesn't belong here.

You're on the Rafter W ranch and in our line cabin. I came on you and four guys having an argument last night. After some discussion, they left and you stayed to get repairs. That's about it."

The gun lowered, but Spud noticed it was still pointing in his general direction. "I see. I remember those four. We got into that argument you talked about and nothing else. You the one who sewed up my face?"

"Yeah, it'll look a lot better in a week or so. Can you move your jaw? Guess so, you're talking."

"It's getting' easier. My head feels like it's going to bust, and what's keeping me from moving without fire bursting out?"

"Ma'am might be time to put up that hog leg. Don't like to have a gun pointin' at me!"

"Not sure I care what you like, cowboy. I'm not lettin' anyone get the better of me again!"

"I can see why you'd feel ...." Spud took the gun from her hand before she could move. Pain exploded on her face. "Now, that's better. Hope that didn't hurt your ribs too bad. That's what hurts so bad when you move. You'll have to be easy for maybe four or five weeks maybe. I'll go into town tomorrow and get the doctor to come look at them. We'll know better then. How about some coffee? Think you could swallow?"

She had lain down quietly and watched him after losing the gun. Feeling her side, "What keeps me from breathin' in? Did you do something to me?"

"Put bandages on you. We need to keep those ribs from moving. Might push one through your lungs and then you'd be in big trouble."

"You had me naked in here last night?" the fire spitting from her swollen eyes.

"Not naked! I took what was left of your shirt off and put bandages around your ribs and that was it! Didn't do anything that didn't have to be done!"

"You god dammed ignorant cowboy, I hope you got your fill. It's a good thing for you that you got that gun, I'd shoot you for sure now!"

"Think nothing of it, ma'am. Glad to kill two hombre and shoot another to save your hide. You might try getting over your enormous ego; you're not exactly a picture I can't resist. I was able to contain myself and fix you up without abusing any trust my momma put on me."

Moving to the stove, Spud spent some time in silence. Making a fire, putting on the coffee, setting on the skillet to fry some meat he'd cut off a hindquarter all this took some time, and allowed Spud to calm down some. He realized that she was understandably upset and had been through a terrible ordeal. She had the right to be unreasonable. "Do you want that coffee?"

No response was forthcoming. Spud poured two cups full and getting his chair next to the bed sat sipping one and holding the other. "It's still a might hot. We better wait 'til it cools some."

"I'm sorry cowboy." The voice was real quiet. "After what you did for me, that's the last thing you deserve. I'm real sorry and thank you very much.

That horrible brute was going to kill me as sure as the sun rises. I'm alive today and hurting because you were brave and rescued me and I go and cuss you out for it. Hope you can forgive me."

Spud blew on his coffee cup and avoided looking at her.

"Already have. Figured you were a bit not responsible for what you said. Sure glad I got that gun before you went off the deep end though."

"Yeah, could have done a terrible thing. Being sorry afterwards wouldn't have helped. Well, again, I'm sorry and thanks! That coffee looks and sounds good but how am I ever going to drink it. Maybe I can set up if I go real slow."

"Not a good idea. We can't move those ribs."

"They feel like you wrapped them up real tight. Help me lift my legs and swing them over and we'll see what that feels like."

Working slowly, they tried to get her to a set up position but failed. Spud had seen some tough cowboys but he was impressed by the pain she took and was grateful she finally decided to quit trying. Lying back with sweat on her brow, "Maybe you'll have to spoon feed me for a while."

Spud put spoonfuls into her busted lips until the cup was gone. "Do you think you could chew some meat now that we got you warmed up?"

"Not really! It hurts my jaw to just swallow. Do you think it's busted?"

"No, I didn't think so. I felt along your jawbone and your face and couldn't find anything. We had a puncher who broke his jaw once and you're not like that at all. I think you're just bruised and sprained. I think you're just so light you moved when he hit you rather than break. We can take it easy today and maybe tomorrow you can chew real slow."

"Ok!"

Spud ate his breakfast and washed the skillet. Think I'll saddle and take a look around. This is the first time I been here and I need to get the lay of the land so to speak."

"Are you sure those men are gone! What if they come back?"

"Yeah they're gone! I followed their tracks this morning. That's where I was coming back from when you tried to shoot me. I think I put lead in one of them and if I did they aren't going to be very combative for a while. You'll be all right. I'll let you have the gun back if you'll promise not to shoot me when I come back."

"Alright, if you think that's best. I'll just nap while you're gone."

Placing the pistol by her head, "That's the best thing for you."

Chapter Eight

Spud spent several hours on a clear, crisp beautiful
morning looking over his winter charge. The cows were
fat, the ponds full and all was well. He had decided
instead of going into town for a doctor and the sheriff, he
would fix a lock for the door. At least if anything
happened he would have time to point a gun before they
got in.

If he knew that woman, it would be two guns
pointed at intruders. At least he could get some sleep
tonight; he was showing the effects of all the excitement.

Pulling the big roan's saddle off and whipping him
off, he set about finding what he would need. There was a
handsaw in the lean-to barn and some wood he could use

stacked beside the cabin. He went to look at the door to design his latch. Knocking several times. "It's me Ma'am. I'm coming in."

She was lying on her back. "Hi! Did you look around?"
"I'll say. Those are the fattest cows I've ever seen. There's grass enough here to feed all of Texas's. Everything looked just fine, so I decided to put a bar on this door.

Maybe I can get some sleep if I can get it so someone can't just walk in." Spud set about getting his door barred.

"I got up while you were gone. All I could do was walk around by the bunk and then I had to stop, but I got up. Maybe this evening I'll get up again, it won't be long before I'm able to get by." She paused, "Tell me what happened last night after I passed out. Did you tell me that two of them was killed? My name is Elsa Shepard."

"Whoa!" Spud put down the lumber," You must be feeling a lot better. Hi, Elsa! My name's Spud Turner. Well, I was coming up here to set up our winter camp and saw lights. Decided that it was best to check it out first, so I sneaked up and heard you getting your brains beat out.

I went in with the drop on everyone and told them to disarm. The big fellow smacked the lamp, I shot at him and then all hell broke loose.

The fellows that got killed was during that. I put a bullet in one other guy and I was sure that it was the big guy. Don't know how I could have missed him but he was riding just fine when they took off down the valley."

"Humph! You couldn't hurt that filthy, viscous pig with just a bullet. Hope you killed him! What did the dead ones look like?"

"Yeah, never thought of that. He was big enough to take a bullet wasn't he? I sure shot him from real up close. Maybe he could ride with it in him. One dead guy was middle aged, bearded and kind of tall and skinny. Know which one he is?"

"Sure, glad you killed him. Did they take the black?"

"The Horse? That's right! That was the same bunch I saw crossing the creek day before yesterday. Don't know why I didn't recognize that horse. The big guy was on him but they left pretty much ever' thing else. Got their saddles and skedaddled out of here."

"Oh, you're kidding! Spud is it? Would you please look and see if they left my saddlebags behind?"

"Sure, which one's yours?"

"Elsa looked funny laying real still on her back and talking without moving anything. "It's the one that looks new. Sort'a brown while everyone else's is like dirt and oil."

Pulling it from the pile in the corner, "Yeah here it is. Want anything from it. Sure is heavy."

"Oh, Heavens, open it up and see if my money's still there."

"Damn, it sure is. This yours?"

She didn't answer right away. "This makes it bad. They won't go anywhere without that. They know it's here."

"Sure puts new boots on it alright. But if you think about it one of them's got lead in him and that's not ever easy. I bet the other one's got his hands full taking care of the wounded. Course I guess he could leave him to get along as best he can and come back by himself."

"He wouldn't do anything without that bucket of scum telling him he could. They don't even breathe without asking Al Hartwig if they can first. Al's not going to let him come back without him. Let's say you hit him solid. If he doesn't die when will he be well, do you think?"

"Hard to say, couple' a months anyway I'd think!" Pausing, "How'd they get you anyway?"

"Woke up in the middle of the night, and they were all over me. Couldn't do a thing about it and I've been living in hell ever since. If you hadn't decided to jump in, they would've killed me before very long. I know I was wantin' it to be soon. So, thank you forever Spud. I owe you!"

"Anybody a' done it. Guess they deserved it, then."

"You're not feelin' bad about hurting them are you? Believe me Spud; I've seen rattlesnakes that were better than those four. You done the whole world a favor and I hope they see the fires of Hell before I draw another breath!"

"Can't say as I blame you for that. We'll get the sheriff after them tomorrow."

"The sheriff? Oh, we can't do that."

"Yeah, we'll have to tell him about the dead guys!"

"There's nobody going to miss them. Why stir things up? Just leave it alone, I'll be on my way before the others can get back and you'll be down at the ranch house. They won't even know what you look like. No need to complicate things, don't you think?"

"No, you've got to report a killin'. The Rafter W sure can't have a killing on its place without reporting it. So, you see, it's really not up to me. I'll have to let June know too."

"Set down for a minute would you Spud? I need to talk to you."

Pulling up a chair and putting the bags on her bunk, "What's up Ma'am?"

"I can see you're dead set on telling everybody about this and I don't want everyone to know what happened. Maybe if you could just wait a couple of days until I can get on a horse. I'll be gone and you can tell them then. That's not so bad is it?"

"No! That's not so bad except you're not going to be up in a day or two. You're not thinkin' that what happened is your fault or that you have to be ashamed or anything?"

"What do you think? They were raping me! Do you hear me, cowboy, over and over again. Those filthy pigs! It makes me sick even thinking about it."

Spud reached out to touch her motionless hand. "Miss Elsa that don't have nothin' to do with you. They did that themselves and they have all the blame. Not you! As soon as you heal up, you'll be as good as new. Don't you worry about what anyone thinks about you! Ain't nobody goin' to put any of this on you. We just need to get them behind bars so's they can't do this to someone else."

"No! I couldn't stand that! We need to wait. I can be gone in just a little time. I can ride almost today. By tomorrow I should be able to make it."

"No, Ma'am. You'll be able to make it to the outhouse maybe. That'll be about it." Spud sat looking at his new acquaintance for a while. "Maybe it's time you told me about why you're out on this lonesome prairie with all that money by yourself."

"Why! If I was a man you wouldn't even think of asking me that question. It's none of your business what I do with my life. That's my money and what I was doing is my business. I certainly don't have to clear it with you before I decide what to do with my life."

"Yes, Ma'am. All that's sure true. Ever' thing you said's true but now I have the feeling that your story is a lot more complicated than what we've talked about so far." After a brief pause, "I think I'd better find out the whole story. Fellow needs to be careful about what he gets mixed up in. I was thinkin' that we was just ordinary but now maybe it's not so ordinary. Why don't you fill me in on the whole story before we go any farther?"

"You're asking me to take you into my confidence when I don't even know you. How could I do that?"

"Well, it's for sure we ain't known each other long but I know you pretty well. I think you know me pretty well. Besides I'm involved whether we like it or not. I figure I got a right and I know I'm not goin' any farther without knowing the whole story."

She did her best to glare at him. It wasn't very effective. If you could see her face it was almost funny if it hadn't been horrible.

"You're going to do what if I don't tell you things you have no right to know?"

"Guess I'd have to go get the authorities to settle this out. There's been a crime committed and someone needs to get to the bottom of this. If I can't, I'll have to find someone who can."

"Fine! If you need to know my private business so much I'll tell you. I left my husband and took that money when I left. It was mine as much as his, wasn't it?"

"Sure! So you figure the laws after you for stealing?"

"Oh, there's been a complaint made. You can bet on it."

"That's not a worry. We can get the sheriff to fix that without you even having to go back. Married folk have communal property. I doubt if he could even get a warrant at all. You're just worryin' about nothing. Shoot that's not so bad at all."

"So now you're actually a lawyer and the poor little lady's out of her head. Well thanks so much for your unasked for opinion. I'm not about to take a chance of winding up back there."

After a brief pause, "So you decide to leave your husband and this forces you to take off across the wilderness by yourself? That don't make sense Ma'am. Seems to me your leavin' something out. We need to have the truth here. Can't come to the right answer without it."

"Why don't you just beat it out of me? Here I am helpless, can't even get up and you're bullying me."

"Wish ya' hadn't said that. No need to try working me Ma'am. I'm just natcherly immune to it. It's time. Stop stallin' and come up with the truth or I'm through."

"No don't do that! I've told you the truth. Well, almost!" She paused, "Oh, fine, my husband was dead when I left him. That's all. Feels almost good to tell someone, even you! I shot him, the bully! And, I'd do it again! He was beating me senseless and I shot him for it. Told him not to touch me again and now he never will."

"Oh! Well if that don't beat all? You married this fellow and he started beating you? If you don't mind my askin' what is it about you that makes everyone start to hit you?"

"I do mind! Maybe it's just because I don't bend down and kiss their mighty butt. Did you ever think of that?"

"Can't say I have. So, you think there's a warrant out on you for his killing? Is that it?"

"Oh, his daddy owns half of Chicago. He's got half of Cook county out after me, you can bet on it. The way I look at it I didn't do anything wrong. What man would be arrested if he killed another man who was beating him up?

None, you know it's true. Plenty of men have been ruled justified homicide for the same exact thing. But a wife just has to go on letting him build up his ego by punching her around. He'd go to work and let his daddy chew him out and then come home and take it out on me. I'm not sorry and I'm not going to let anyone put me in jail for it."

"Whoa! Knew there was something but this is a lot more than I ever expected. We got a real problem here. Oh, don't look at me that way! I'm not bailin'. Said I think

I know you pretty well and I do. Don't think there's anything bad about you!

It's just, well, how are we going to take care of this? Guess I could quit here and take you where you're going. We could just not tell the sheriff about you. He doesn't need to know the whole story to put out a warrant on them. I could just tell him that I hailed the cabin and all hell broke loose. Does that sound good?"

"Are you thinking that I'm going to take up with you just because you're willing to help me?"

Spud couldn't help laughing, "I'm going to have to get you a mirror. You're going to have to get a lot better lookin' before you stand a shot with me. I's just thinkin' how best to work this out so's everyone comes out on top.

I'll ask again if you think that would work. It'd buy us some time for you to heal. Then, we'd let Mr. Wilson know I was shakin' it. Damn, I hate to do that. Told him I wasn't a saddle tramp and would sign on for the duration. Well, this is more important. You got a right to be happy, just like everyone else. Where were you going?"

"So, I'm not good enough for some ignorant cowboy, eh? Take a while to get used to that. At one time every man I saw wanted me, oh well. Even if you don't think I'm much to look at, I think you're just too good to be true. Why would you throw over your life just to help some poor women that life hadn't been treating very well lately?"

"Now, I'm not sayin' you're an ugly women at all. You're just beat up is all. In a couple of weeks that'll be all healed and a fellow can see you'd be right pretty when all that swellin' goes down. I just thought it was funny when you said that is all. Could we talk about what we're going to do now?"

"You'd feel better talking about more manly things? Like what to do instead of women's things. Uh?"

"Guess I was kind'a uncomfortable."

There was a long pause with both parties staring off into space. "Tell you what I think Mr. Spud Turner. I think I'm tired. We don't have to solve the problem right now. Why don't you finish your door and I'll snooze. Then, I'll get up and see if I can make it around here some. We'll sleep on it tonight and decide what's best tomorrow morning. How's that sound?"

Spud smiled at her. "A good manly plan if I ever heard one."

Chapter Nine

She had been stirring for a long time before Spud had even moved. Her legs were moved off the bed, and she had set up and stood up before his highness made the sounds that meant he would be wide awake like a jack-in-the-box before long. You'd never seen anybody that woke up exactly like he did! Wham! He was bolt upright, but back to the girl. She was obviously in great pain.   By moving slowly and steadily she had made it to the bench and was seated when Spud popped up and gave his best impression of an owl.

"Good Morning! You feeling better?"

"Breathing and moving's a problem. I think I'm even worse than I was yesterday, but I'm up."

After stretching out to his full length, twisting in both directions and making a huge yawn, Spud got up and moved toward the stove. "Yeah, today should be your worst day if past experience proves right. I remember this hombre that was hurt a lot like you.

He got into it with this rougher from a stage line. His bruises started to let up on the third day. The second, it was like he just started to move a little and he hurt like the blazes. If you can make it through today, tomorrow should be better."

"Glad to hear it!"

There was no more talk as Spud busied himself making his fire. He tore out several pages from the female section of the Monkey Ward catalog and laid several small sticks in tepee fashion over the wadded-up pages.

Striking and applying his match, he watched as the flame engulfed his carefully laid structure. Thinking how he loved to watch a flame, Spud started to lay bark and larger sticks onto the leaping flames.

"You'll feel better when you've had your coffee. Shouldn't be long now!"

"Good! Can't come too soon!"

Spud set the burner cover back on the stovetop and readied his coffee pot. Setting it on the stove, he sat on the opposite side of the table and viewed his handy work. She looked a fright.

"Hadn't we better talk about what we're going to do?"

"I really appreciate the 'we' part of that. No matter what else happens I can't tell you what a relief it is to have someone take my side for a change. I thought about it before I dropped off last night and it's sure been a long time since that happened.

My Mom wanted me to be a better wife and that would cure my problems. My Dad just wanted the job my husband gave him so he could take care of the rest of the family and my wonderful husband was just an awful man (not to mention his family).

Those four pigs just go without sayin'. So, you see, it's been a while, and it feels real good. I just wanted you to know.

After she had paused, "I also thought about what to do. I need to get somewhere out of the reach of my ex-father-in-law. That's about it. My life don't need anything before that. If you will help me, I think I can be a lot happier than I've managed to be so far. I can pay you your salary. I'll hire you right now and give you a job until we reach California and give you a bonus to get you back to here. How does that sound?"

"Well, I was thinking more about how to solve our immediate problem, like what story to tell the sheriff. As far as a salary, I was about to leave the great mass of salaried workers and buy a place of my own. So I can pretend I left early and I won't need a salary. This job was just a place filler until spring came. Since you have that stash, you can pay for our expenses but that's about all of a problem we should have about money.

What story would be best to tell? I still think we should just leave you out. I can say that I saw a light, left the horses to look and they pulled leather when I opened the door. What'd ya' think?"

"That story makes sense to me. What questions do you think they would ask?"

"Hum! Maybe who drew first and how the fight went. You know, who got shot and like that."

"Well, what're the answers to those?"

"I'll just tell the truth. That's always best. We're just hiding you for good reasons. So we can't tell them about you but the rest can be truth."

"Ok! So then we wait a week or so and set out?"

"It'll be more than a week but yeah."

"How long do you think?"

"Well there's no reason to start until you're strong enough to finish. Say about a month, maybe?"

The coffee pot was boiling too fast so Spud moved to push it onto a cooler part of the stove top, "Today I'll take the bodies in to the ranch and see what Mr. Wilson wants done."

"I can be ready before a month. We better get started before really cold weather sets in."

"That's true. Maybe it would be best to wait until spring before we set out."

Well, we can think about that and decide later, can't we?"

After a brief silence, "How does that coffee sound?" Moving to the stove, Spud got two cups down.

"Not sure anything could be better."

Spud finally got the rancid bodies on their horses. After only two days the smell still made him want to throw up. Several times he had to stop himself from actually gagging. He kept telling himself that he didn't have to eat them. Just get them to the authorities and he would be free of them.

Mounting the gray, he left the little cabin thinking of the women he was leaving behind. She had to be feeling better about her situation now. Her life had been a nightmare that few would ever experience the like of. Spud was sure he would never have been able to handle something like that with the same frankness that she had apparently been able to.

Well, Spud decided to help in some small way if he could. It would be little enough. Maybe two months and he would be back on track to take care of his own dreams knowing that he had helped someone who had something good coming to them.

Chapter Ten

The sound of a hammer sticking an anvil could be heard across the prairie long before the buildings came into view. Since he had left the gravel bed of the road there had been grass up to his horse's belly. What cow country this must be? Spud came to the shoe barn first and stopped as Pete hobbled around on one crutch to raise his hand in greeting. "What's you doin' down here Spud? Somethin' wrong?"

"Had a bit of trouble, Pete. Nothin' serious. How's that leg? Looks like you're getting around better than when I saw you last."

"Yeah, pain's gone kinda. Doc says to just keep my weigh off it and that it's healing just like it should. What kind' a trouble you have? What in the hell is that smell?"

"Killed these bundles on Big Red. Came down to let Mr. Wilson know and take them in to the sheriff if Mr. Wilson says to."

"Don't say! Be damned! You some kind' a gun hawk or what? Don't think I missed that move you put on ol' Stick a while back. I'm the only one who noticed but it was real smooth. Kind' a figured to file it away to a time I might need it myself. Just take your hat off is that it? Well, let me get mounted and we'll find the ol' Man. He's around the house somewhere's. Can't wait to hear this story!"

They found Mr. Wilson in the mess hall with a stack of papers spread out around him and a cup of coffee.

"Howdy Boss, needed to let you know about some trouble at the line camp when I got there night before last."

"Don't say! What happened?"

"Ran into four gents squattin' in the cabin. Saw some light in the cabin so I left the horses back and walked up. Opened the door and asked what they were doing there and all hell broke loose.

Killed two and put lead in one more. The two that was still moving lit out and went down the road toward Cheyenne. Spent yesterday looking around and everything seemed right so I brought the dead ones to find out what you wanted done."

"Damn! Boy are you all right?"

"Yeah, I got off the first shot and the lamp gutted out. In the dark you couldn't hit a wall, so it was pretty much over. They ran out the door and shucked it on down the road. They left most of their stuff so I brought it in too."

"Glad you're ok. Hate to get a man killed in his first week. Why don't you two get some coffee and sit down? We'll decide what to do."

After everybody settled Mr. Wilson offered, "Don't see anything to do. You did what you had to do and you had every right to challenge them. Them being on our property an' all. Guess we better take the bodies on into the sheriff. Boys like that's probably wanted anyway.

Might be you could get some money out of this Spud. I'd put up good money myself that they's a reward on them. Gent that doesn't even want to talk before killing has to be wanted. He's spooky from watchin' his back trail for so long. You two got any ideas?"

Both shook their heads. "Ok! Let's finish our coffee and we can head out. Spud why don't you hitch up the team and Pete and I'll ride in with you? You want to go, Pete?"

"Oh yeah! I got two months to finish making those shoes. No need to get in a hurry now. Besides, I can't get enough of this story. Aint he something there boss? First Stick and now this little blowup in less than a week, we might have a interesting winter after all. Cain't wait to hear every bit about this."

Every time they moved the body the stench rose up to gag both Mr. Wilson and Spud but they finally got them in the wagon wrapped in the slicker Spud had used. With the outlaws' horses tied to the tailgate and Spud mounted they set off for town.

"You probably never killed anyone before have you Spud?"

"No, sure enough not. Not even close before. In fact some people would tell you that I go out of my way to avoid trouble. Have even been one or two gents that at least once voiced concerns about my courage. This just came on real sudden."

"Yeah, it sure happens that way. Been in more than a few of them myself. Why I'm talking to you now. Ever onc't in a while I count up the ones I've planted even though I hate doin' it. They kind'a haunt me in a way. Come to me when I really don't want them to. How you feelin' about this now that you've had some time to think on it?"

"Ahh! I haven't shed any tears over them. They's sure going to kill me if I had just stood there, and if you could have seen them you'd know they were bad men. I don't think about it at all. Pretty sure I did everyone a favor."

They rode in silence to the sheriff's office. With his direction they took the body to the undertaker and were all three seated in front of Sheriff Thompson's desk as he thumbed through a stack of papers from his file cabinet.

"Who'd you shoot first?"

"This big bear of a man moved first so I shot him. That's when the lights went out and everyone started shooting."

147

"How'd you get this hombre? Just shoot him in the dark?"

"No, actually I bumped into him in the dark. I plugged him then, I think."

"You put lead in another one. Did you shoot him when they run?"

"No, I let 'em go when they started to run. I think I hit him by firing at his muzzle flash before I bumped into the dead one."

"The big guy you plugged was riddin' fine though?"

"Yeah! Just lookin' at him, I'd say he was fine but I don't see how I could have missed him. Maybe I just got a piece of him and it was nothing serious."

"This look like him?" Pulling a page from the stack of papers he had been thumbing through, He handed Spud a picture of the outlaw.

"That's the big one. Sure enough."

"We'll need to wait until I get a physical description from Mr. Wood, he does the county coroner work, to be sure but this is him or at least it sure looks like him. And, here's the other one. You're right, Sam, they's as bad as they come. Wanted for murder in Arkansas and Missouri.

The big guy you shot must be Al Hartwig. Says here that this Stewart rode with him the last report.

All of them are wanted in Arkansas for questioning on armed robbery and murder of a bank clerk. I'd say you was either awful good or ridin' with God on your side. You faced some bad men, sonny! If it is this here Stewart he's got five hundred dollars on his head comin' to you. The other's worth two hundred so you made a pretty penny for short work. We'll have to wait until I hear back from the sheriff in Arkansas but it looks like you're going to be paid for your bravery."

"Hot damn, Spud, you're a rich man! When you think he can get it Sheriff? I'll be in town this weekend, I could pick it up for him then."

"Not that soon, Pete, maybe in a couple a' weeks or so at the soonest. I'll sell their stuff and pay for the funeral out of that. You get the rest. If the bodies of the other two show up, you'll have even more.   That Hartwig had a thousand on his head alone. They sure want him bad."

"That's all right Sheriff. You can just put it in the bank when it comes. No need for anyone to bother about it. I'll tell Mr. Vance to expect it and he can take care of it for me."

"You got money in the local bank?"

"Yeah. Hope that's all right Boss. Opened up an account the day I rode out to see you."

"All right? It's great! Here I had you figured for a saddle tramp and you got stock in the local bank. Sure sorry for my misjudgment!"

"I tol' you Boss, that's fine. Lookin' at the nag I was ridin' would have made me come to the same conclusion. It didn't bother me and everything worked out. If we're finished here, think I'll go over to the store and buy some stuff and get on back. Barely had time to get a good look around."

"Sure, good work young man. I'll be up with that pie soon."

Spud thought he would get some stuff for Elsa and get on back to see how she was.

Chapter Eleven

Spud had climbed over the low, rugged pass when he left town and dropped down to the lush valley from the northeast. Cutting across the creek, he climbed up to the ridge that ran behind the cabin on the southwest side to check for anything out of the ordinary. Finding nothing amiss, he dropped down on the trail that led from the road and came upon the little cabin. She was down at the lodge pole corral watching the horses when he came into view. Pulling up and dismounting by the lean-to that served as a barn Spud strolled in her direction.

"You must be feeling a lot better!"

"I'm getting around better. They left my mare. That's my horse, I'm glad those animals left her. I only took that Black to spite that old man! I never really liked him even though he could run like the wind. He won a lot of stake races around Chicago. They can have him as long as my mare's here."

"She's a fine looker. Looks pretty fast herself."

"Well, she's not the Black but she's alright. It's her personality that's really great. She sure tries to please and I treasure that in her. I thought they'd take her. She's a lot better than what they had. It made me sick, thinking of her in their filthy hands as sweet as she is."

"I know what you mean. In the end, attitude is always the most important. Your bruises on your face are turning all different colors. That's good! Means they're healing. Do your ribs feel like they're stable and not moving around?"

"Stable?"

"Yeah, you'd expect that they'd still hurt when you move but we'd have to do something if they seem to be moving."

"Oh, then I think they're all right. Surely they hurt like the blazes every time I think about moving but I think that's all they do. I'm going to be fine as soon as I heal up. What did your boss say?"

"Nothing! Said I needed to challenge them since they were on our range and that they were probably outlaws since they started shooting so sudden like. Turned out he was right.

The sheriff found some fliers on them and they're all wanted men. The gent I killed was wanted for murder and the whole gang is wanted for bank robbery and murder of a bank clerk. That big one has a thousand dollars on his head!"

"Sure wish you could collect on him. The idea of worms eating on his rotten flesh makes me real happy."

"I can understand that! Got you some stuff when I was in town. Hope you like them."

"You got me something! What is it?"

The emotion in her voice made Spud look in time to see the tears before she wiped her face, "Yeah, it's not much. Got you a coat, a hat and some gloves. Then I got you a scarf that looked real pretty. Hope you like them. I'll take care of my horse and start supper. You can look at them when you get back to the cabin."

Spud unsaddled, brushed and grained the Grey and left Elsa leaning against the poles gazing at the horses. The beans were warmed and the steaks almost done when Elsa came shuffling into the cabin and struggled to her seat. Spud dished up their meal and set her plate and himself down. They ate in silence and Spud retrieved a package when they had both finished. He pulled a sheepskin coat out and held it up.

"Does that look like it'll fit you?"

"It's beautiful. I think it'll fit fine!"

"I got us both wool stocking hats. George said they were best. These gloves are the small size. I thought your hands were small and here's the scarf. It looked real pretty to me. You can try all this on and if it don't fit I'll take it in and get the right size before it gets any colder. I also got you a new shirt to replace the one that got torn. I'll put all this stuff on your bunk"

"Did you ever notice how life evens out, Spud? It just kind'a goes along with nothing good or bad happening. Then maybe something good happens but something bad will happen to even it out.

In the end most of us have a life that's all evened out. I just want you to know that you're wiping out a lot of bad things lately. Thanks for all this."

"I figure you got a lot of good coming to you before you get even. We'll just wait here 'til you're ready and then get you somewhere that you'll get along good."

"Tell me Spud what did you tell the storekeeper you were buying women's sized clothes for?"

"I just told him they were for my gal back home. That I was going to take them to her when I went back."

"Oh, so you've got a girl-back-home do you?"

"Well kind'a. Nothin's been said for sure but Wanda and I have an understanding of a sort."

"Understandin'?"

"Well, yeah! Like something's goin' to happen sometime."

"You scoundrel! You've got her waiting, hoping that something's going to happen? She should be asking for more than that to wait all this time for you."

"Now, she's not all that poorly. She's about the prettiest thing in two counties and her daddy owns a nice spread. She's got plenty of gents lookin' to spoon her. If she needs, she can go to any one of them. I've just got other things to take care of first, is all."

You'd think she was smiling, but you couldn't tell really. What with the swelling an' all.

Chapter Twelve

She'd had a useful mirror when she had first set out, but now she had only salvaged a small portion of it as it had been broken during her 'troubles'. It was a large enough piece to illuminate portions of her face. Elsa studied each wound on her appearance and noted the changes as they developed.

Every blow had produced a wound, and each wound was all swollen and red after two days. Spud's stitches, while functional, made railroad tracks over what had been a lovely face by all accounts previously. Her entire face looked as though it would burst if pressed too hard, and deep red was the prevalent color.

Today the color had changed considerably. It was a shade toward purple, but the swelling still made her look like it would explode.

The wounds looked like a knot had formed inside. Spud assured her that this was good. He said her body was fighting off the infection from her wounds. That sounded good to Elsa.

Day by day, she noticed no perceptibly change in confort but she did more each day. At first, it was just getting around the cabin. She started doing cleaning in the cabin. She got out to the horses for a time and back.

She undertook the repair of furniture in the cabin. A leg for the table was carved out of a limb with much pain. Swinging the ax to cut the limb down hurt beyond counting, but the table had broken when her body was propelled against it with great force and she was pleased to repair it herself. The lean-to needed some chinks filled and boards replaced so she undertook this next.

After two weeks of this there was no perceptable change in appearance, but she had persuaded Spud that she could go to work with him and she had worked cattle all morning before she retired to the cabin for the afternoon.

She thought she might look a little better. Maybe the swelling had gone down some. For sure she could work part of the day without a break.

She thought she might look a little like herself and her ribs had not hurt her all day. This cattle stuff was fun!

The stitches had broken on the largest wound on her face today. It had bled some but not a lot. Spud thought none of her wounds needed to be re-stitched. He decided that the one that had opened would be fine, so Elsa did not worry about it.

A new scab had formed over the one that had bled yesterday and it looked fine.

Elsa put her mirror away and just worked this day.

Spud had just run two bulls and a heifer down from the north-east ridgeline and was sitting his gray watching Elsa and her mare work the southwest slope. They were working three young heifers that were spry and presenting a considerable challenge.

Three weeks had rushed by so fast that they seemed to be all one instant. The events almost melted together but the pair had settled into a routine that grew as if it had sprung whole. The pair found that their youth gave them a common bond and wound up spending the time from supper to their separate beds lost in conversation.

Now, Spud marveled at the workmanship shown by the young lady and her horse. At the outset of their relationship Spud had watched with extreme earnestness for evidence about Elsa's character but now doubts were gone. If watching Elsa with her horse had been all that he had done, that would have been enough to convince him of her goodness. It was a lot more than that. Her very being had proven to him that she was an angel.

Spud had always been a happy person. He thought that it started with his parents, who kept things light around the two boys. Skinny and he had talked many times about keeping a positive view of the future. They both knew and disliked cowboys who were always cantankerous and hostile. They both felt it better to just be happy.

It was never like this. The joy of getting up in the morning, working all day, and talking the evening away had never compared to this. It was as if the world had been in black and white but was now in color.

That night in the cabin that he had agreed to help her and had said that he knew her, had been correct. He did know her. How in the world those two men back in Chicago had driven her to the extreme she had admitted was beyond Spud. Surely they had been horrible people.

Probably they were members of the rich who looked at the world as composed of betters and those not as worthy. Since they were rich and powerful, they knew they belonged to the group that was better because they deserved to. They surely lacked respect for others. Well, she didn't have to live like that any longer.

Going out every day to work the herd with someone like Elsa had proven a joy. What with being a city girl and only a few weeks or so working on horseback the horse and riders' ability was astounding.

Spud watched as horse and rider performed as one. The heifers would spin to go back uphill and they would be cut off and forced to resume moving down toward the valley floor.

You had to hand it to her. She was a natural athlete to accomplish that in so short a time. When horse and rider melded into one, you had a working unit. She sure looked good doing it too. It was becoming all too apparent why she had said that men paid attention to her.

The wounds were healing and the knots were shrinking, molding her face back into a work of art. Spud found that he was spending a lot of his time watching her as she moved and enjoying it a great deal.

Well, they would finish their first complete swing through the valley ridges and all showed good. For late fall the grass was still green and lush.

Spud had decided that the ranch could be run better. The line shacks could be used as summer range and then the stock pushed down to the lower valley where the grass could be cut and stacked for winter-feed. Maybe he could talk to June sometime, see why they did it this way.

They just spread them out all over their range. The stock and range were in great shape though and the winter was only to be waited on. Just keep them pushed down into the valley and patrol the area. Pretty lazy days if compared to round up.

They would get back to the line cabin early today and Spud thought that a couple of days off before making their second sweep to run stock down to the valley floor was a good idea. He would have to think of some reward to celebrate. Maybe just take the time off, get a bath and rest. He swung the gray up the slope to finish off the day's work.

They had edged up to the cut-bank and were prepared to let the horses pick their way down to the rocky creek bed when Spud noticed the two new horses in the corral.

Ice spread through Spud's veins, as his first reaction was one of caution. Before he could yank the reins around and force his horse back from view, he saw his boss sitting on a coral pole looking in their direction. Without breaking stride, "Mr. Wilson's here!"

"The owner?"

"Yeah! See him on the coral?"

"Uh hu. He's an old man?"

"He's getting' there. Still moves well and seems like a real nice person. I know his men think the world of him."

The horses were moving in the rocky creek bed and Spud lost her reply. They moved up the closer bank and hailed Mr. Wilson. Who waved back and lit on his feet to stroll in their direction.

"Howdy there Mr. Wilson! Good to see you."

Howdy Spud! Brought that pie we talked about. Hope it's big enough for three of us."

"Yeah, sounds good. This here's Miss Elsa Shepard, Mr. Wilson. She's stayin' with us for a while."

"I see! Howdy Miss. Shepard. Welcome to the Rafter. That's a fine mount you have there. Like to have me help you with the saddle?"

"Thanks, but I've got it. Got hurt a while back and I need to keep movin' til it heals. You're right about her. She's getting' work for the first time in her life and I think she loves it.

"Sure? Then I'll stroll up to the cabin. See you there!"

"Oh, No! What're we goin' to tell him?"

"Nothin' to say but the truth. If that's not good enough we'll have to pull out.

They had finished their chores with the horses in silence and found Wilson seated at the crude plank table. "So, what brings you to our neck of the woods, Miss Shepard?"

"Sounds funny to hear the Miss. Why don't you call me Elsa? I'm afraid I was brought here against my will and have been recovering from injuries since then."

Spud spoke up, "I probably owe you this explanation, Sam. You see I didn't tell the whole story about those galoots that were in the cabin when I got here."

"Did you lie Spud?"

"Well I didn't tell you anything that wasn't true but I also didn't tell you everything. The part I left out was about them having taken this young lady captive and their abusing of her when I arrived. She asked me to keep that part about what happened to her a secret and I did that. Hope you don't hold that against me. Just did what I felt was best."

"Oh, don't blame Spud. It was all me. I just couldn't stand having people know what had happened and Spud was kind enough to keep my little secret. We talked about it and decided that it wouldn't hurt anyone and would help me face people after I healed."

"Boy, you never know what a day will bring. I thought I was old enough to have seen it all, but this is new. I guess I can see why you would be embarrassed about your experience young lady, but you're selling the people in this territory short by a long ways.

We've had those who were taken by injuns and were welcomed back into our community. They didn't do anything wrong by our standards and neither did you. I can tell by lookin' that you've had it bad an' the Rafter W would be honored to have you here. It's not much but you're welcome to what we have."

"That's very kind of you Mr. Wilson. You're just as Spud said you were, but I'm planning on leaving here soon. I think I'm strong enough now but Spud says a couple of weeks longer."

"That's something else we need to talk about Mr. Wilson. I've decided that I'm not going to let her take off by herself. That didn't work out too well last time she tried it and there's no reason to expect any better this time. So, I'm thinkin' of asking to be released from my word to finish out this winter with you and plan on helpin' Elsa on to California before headin' on back to Texas."

"Seems to me that any man who wouldn't do that wouldn't be fit to have his salt given to'em. Fact is I might go with you just to help. Are you set on going all the way out there Miss, er, Elsa?"

"Yes, Sir, I have family out there. My husband died and they're all I have."

"I see! Well, we can sure help you with that and be glad to do it. If I could offer some advice though, I would say that you can't leave now.

You'd never make it. I've been that way and there're some very tall mountains in the way. Most of the way is going to hold the potential for weather that would kill you if you're out in it."

"I knew it was winter between here and there but I didn't know it was that bad."

"Yeah, it is! You start climbing just west of here and you don't go down until you hit fourteen thousand feet in California. You just can't get through until the spring. Ya' got no chance a'tol of making it til then."

"Sounds like we'll need to wait, Elsa. Thanks for the advice Sam. We'd have taken off like pilgrims and been in a world of hurt."

"Sure 'nuff, young man. What do you think Miss Elsa?"

"Please, just Elsa. I wanted to get on out there but if we can't we can't."

"I use the Miss not for respect to you but to remind me that I'm an old man. When one gets around someone as attractive as you it's best to keep reminding himself that he's too old to get any ideas."

"Well aren't you sweet! And gallant too! The men on this ranch are just a cut above, that's for sure. I guess there's nothing left but to wait as you've suggested. At least Spud can stop harping about my strength."

The old man's smoothness again impressed Spud as he said, "Yeah, at least I can keep my word about stayin' till spring."

"Then it's settled. Now we have to figure out a change in our living arrangements. It's not decent that you stay up here with Spud. I know the two of you aren't doing anything that's indecent, but we have to think of what's proper."

"I guess I never thought about that. What're we going to do?"

"I was thinkin' that Elsa could come down to the ranch house and stay there. Cookie could use some help with the cookin' and I could always use some help with the books. What do'ya think?"

Elsa's face showed her disappointment, "I like the work here and we're doing real well. We've got one whole swing done and everything is under control. The animals are looked after and we're set up for the cold weather."

"I understand but it's just not possible. We have to consider what people will think."

Spud joined in, "They won't think anything. I'm not ashamed of anything we've done. Everything has been above board and as honest and forthright as could be since I took this job."

"I'm sure you're right. In fact, I know you are, but that's not the point. We've got to consider what people think is appropriate. There are things that most people just don't think is right. We have to take that into account.

I'm sorry you youngsters will just have to do it my way. If you're on rafter we have to be concerned with what passes in the community. I put great store in that and we'll have to follow it."

Taking that as the end of the conversation, Spud got up to build the fire. It had been a short conversation and one that Spud would have sworn would come out different than it had. The Old Man had a way of getting his way.

Things were sure going to change but in the end they would still make it to where Elsa wanted to go and they would do it safely. He would miss her. She sure made the place happier by just being here, but she wouldn't be far away. Besides, he could make excuses for going down to the ranch from time to time.

He wondered how she came up with having relative to go to. It was the one thing that threw Mr. Wilson off.

The last secret they had from him. It wasn't so bad to be apart even though he knew he would miss her, besides all he could think of was that brown, delicious looking pie right now.

Chapter Thirteen

Blacky pulled up his mount. George rode a few more steps before he noticed and he stopped to look back at his friend.

"Let's get on down to the creek before we rest."

"Don't look right! You see anything?"

They were entering some trees that surrounded a deep pool made by a creek that flowed down from the bluffs to the east. Many times in hot weather they would stop to swim but the weather was not hot today.

In fact it was overcast and chilly as the two riders sat their horses and studied the area. They had been nearby and came down to eat lunch before something had alerted Blacky.

"Yeah, looks too open under that group of oaks over there."   George gestured off toward the creek.

"Yeah can't think of any reason 'cept a camp. Don't recon they's someone campin' up here do you?"

"We better check it out. Why don't you swing wide in that direction and I'll go this way. Meet about that cottonwood on the other side."

After a wide circle, Blacky and George pulled up with their stirrups almost touching and their horses faced in the opposite direction. "Yeah. Two horses came in from the meadow and headed where we can see a clearing. Looks like that'll be a camp when we get down to it."

"Well, two took out up that draw, maybe a day or so ago."

"Think they's rustlin'?"

"We better find out! Let's go look at their camp and then we better follow them a ways. If'n they's workin' cattle the tracks'll tell us."

The trail they both followed led them to the bluff behind Spuds cabin and then to another camp. George was the first to talk for some time now, "I just don't see what's goin' on."

"You know what I'm thinkin'? Remember some of those hombres Spud tangled with got away.

Maybe they's come back to continue the battle. Some folks don't know when to let it alone and everyone says they's bad men."

George chewed on that for several miles before he spoke, "That would account for what we seen so far. It sure would have to be one possibility. We better stick to this until we get it figured out. I sure don't like the looks of it."

They toiled on for several hours before Blackie pulled up and got down. Studying the tracks for a while he finally opinioned, "We're still a day behind them. What do you say to the idea that we warn everyone first and then get back on them?"

George pulled out the makings and slowly rolled up a smoke. Blackie had remounted and waited with silence until he spoke. "Yeah, that's the thing to do. If we stay trackin' them, we'll come up on 'um after they done their deed if they'se goin' to do anything. No wonder you lived so long pard. I'll ride back to Spud and let him know. You go tell the boys at the ranch."

Chapter Fourteen

Elsa loved this time of her day. As her mind floated up from the darkness, she could think about the past, the future and the present, and everything in between. Being safe and warm, snuggled within her bedding, made everything possible. Why hadn't he come down? It had been long enough and he should have come in before now.

Not that it was bad here. In fact it was great except for no Spud. All the men at the ranch house had helped to restore her to her normal trusting ways. They had done this by wanting to be her friend. Of course men had always tried to make friends with her but these men were different.

Maybe they did want to crawl into bed with her in the middle of the night but they also had proven to her that they wanted to be friends with her with no strings attached.

That had done a lot in a short time toward improving her self-image. It was like she had gone from hell to heaven. No one had just wanted to be her friend since she had been in school. Just for no reason except that she was worthy of being their friend. Now, she loved someone for the first time since she'd had a schoolgirl crush and had friends to boot.

Boy was Spud going to be surprised when he finds out about all the nice people here. Mr. Wilson was just the kindest man besides Spud she had ever met. Didn't look as good as Spud, though. Blackie the philosopher was always thinking about something important. Like as not he had figured out mans' very existence while half asleep on the back of a horse. June the doer, he got ever thing done with the most gentle of hands. The cows even liked him. Ol' fun-loving Pete put in his contribution to the group. After a month with Spud and a few weeks with these characters, she was about to pronounce herself well.

Lying in bed like this in the morning had become a habit of hers'. Planning out the day and snuggling into the covers was delicious. Get that man of mine down here and it would become ecstatic. She had breakfast to do, and then get busy on figuring out how to mark each head of cattle for her record-keeping project.

Spud would know how to do it. I'll need to tell him that he's in love with me first but really he already knows that. Elsa thought it was funny about people. She had known since she was a little girl that if you watched people as well as listened to them you could really understand them.

There was something about the way they stood, their facial expression or their tone of voice that told a story which augmented what their words said.

Spud was the easiest. He was so sincere that he didn't even know that he was sincere. She had known for weeks that they were in love with each other but she also knew that Spud would go on treating her as if she were a princess unless she did something.

She knew that she could make him the happiest man in the world and had every intention of doing that if only he would get down here. The time she had spent without him had convinced her to act. He just needs to face it and marry me. That's all the options he had, and he better get down here to face the music.

Some noise drifting up from the kitchen made Elsa aware that Cookie was up and at it. Her morning reverie was effectively cut short by the need to work. The clothes that Sam had from his departed wife fit a little large but were fine. Elsa struggled into a full set and hustled downstairs to her first task.

Cookie took care of the fires needed in the kitchen and Elsa lit all the rest in the common space. Splashing ice-cold water in your face could sure send a shiver down your spine but it felt fine.

Drying her hands on the towel, she moved to the stove in the walkway. Last night she had laid the foundation to her fire. Striking her sulfur, she touched the paper at the bottom of her tepee shaped kindling and watched as it caught full flame. She knew that the fire would last for twenty minutes until she could get her coffee.

She could return then to feed larger pieces into the flame. She moved to the stove in the dining room and duplicated her previous chore there.

That done she made her way to the kitchen. Get a quick cup and back to put larger logs on her, by then, well burning fires. As she strode around the doorway expecting to see the little china man at the table she ran smack in front of an ugly ape holding Cookie like he was a doll and pointing a gun at her chest.

"Howdy there, missy. Bet you're glad to see me."

Her heart stopped and moved its position into the back of her throat somewhere.

"Knew that would be you out there singin' in that sweet voice. Well, has the cat got your tongue or you just been missin' me so bad you just can't express yourself now that I'm here?"

"You pig, let him go! There's people all around here and they'll kill you this time. Let him go!"

∞

The morning was cold. Not like it was going to get but still enough to make the warm bed into a haven. June knew that light would be here soon but a few more seconds in the security of warmth seemed like something he needed to cling to. But, there was Elsa and warm coffee over in the kitchen. That was pretty attractive. You add that to Mr. Wilson's glare if you slept too late and the big man was pried out into the day.

Throwing the covers back June let the cold steal in around him. The panel that Cookie had sown into his long johns in order to make them fit was coming unsown and June could feel the cold where it touched his bare skin. For about the twentieth time June promised himself that he would tell Cookie to fix it but he knew it'd be falling off him before he did that.

As he swung his feet over to touch the even colder floor June wanted to know why he couldn't just find clothes to fit himself. Why, just once, he couldn't shift his weight without hearing the creak of the floor. The only time he felt 'normal' was outside. At least the ground didn't complain about his bulk.

Got to quit thinking that way (as he pulled on his trousers). Elsa says a strong, powerful man is attractive to a woman. Can't always be runnin' myself down just for the way I am. That's what Elsa says and lord knows she should know. Nothing had ever been as pretty to him as she was. June let the picture of putting holes in Spud and then seeing if she would come to him play in his mind once more. Be just his luck that ranny up at the line shack would plug him first. Hadn't he done some work on those outlaws? Besides June had been thinking of a Mrs. Johnson back in town since last Saturday.

He stomped into his boots and trudged quickly down the passageway toward the expected warmth of the kitchen and good company. The big man was a mighty quiet walker. Good thing too. As he stepped into the kitchen, all he could see was this huge hole in the end of a gun swinging toward him.

The entire scene yanked itself into him. This big, dirty, ugly cuss who had been holding Cookie in his arms, and pointing a gun at Elsa across the small kitchen was going to shoot him. That scene no sooner became evident than he was shot.

However the scene that was framed in his mind in that instant of awareness did not stay frozen. When the gun was no longer pointing at Elsa, it freed Cookie up to instantly jump the outlaw. He managed to grab Hartwig's wrist before he could fire but the slug still tore into June and he collapsed.

Cookie brought all his weight down on the gun hand of the big outlaw and managed for a moment to almost throw him off balance. The little Chinaman was no match and he probably knew it. He had already made up his mind they were both going to die since Al had said he was going to kill them. June's entrance had just made it possible for him to try to help Elsa. Al regained his balance without much effort and threw the tiny man into the closed door that lead outside.

When June made his unexpected entrance, Elsa did not choose to stay still either. Anticipating the outlaw's move to cover the newcomer, she was already in action before anyone else moved.

Cookie kept a gun on the pantry shelf and that's what she aimed for. Yanking it down from behind the flower sack, she turned, cocked and leveled it at Al

Hartwigs' ugly head. Al had just shot Cookie when her gun discharged a bullet into his head.

Elsa watched as it struck him in the temple and the wall behind him splattered into a splotch of purple red. He dropped like a rock and the sound of him striking the floor had hardly faded away before Elsa could actually feel the quiet.

The scene before her was beyond belief. The smell of gunpowder made her eyes water and her stomach was about to come up. She stumbled a quick step toward the table and, dropping the gun, grabbed a chair with that hand and the table with the other.

That was the only way for her to continue standing. She was in that position wondering why she was the only one still on her feet when Mr. Wilson burst into the doorway.

"Oh, my God, child! Are you all right? What in the name of God has happened?"

"Yeah, I'm ok. I guess everyone else has been shot." The voice seemed to well up from within the sickness she had become.

Kneeling beside June, "God it's June and Cookie. Have they been shot?"

"Yeah! That pile of shit over by the stove shot them. Then I shot him!"

Rising and moving toward her, "My God child, sit down before you fall."

He helped her into the chair she was leaning on, picked up the pistol, and poured her a quick and sloppy cup of coffee before returned to June. With obvious love he rolled him onto his back. Taking out his pocketknife, he cut his shirt and long handles away to reveal the damage.

The wound was on his right side and wasn't bleeding much. Cookie had managed to move the gun off enough to give him a chance. The big man was trying to get his breath and had succeeded in shallow breathing while still unconscious. At least he was still alive.

Turning to Cookie, it took only a quick check to see that he was dead. The large pool of blood and the location of the wound testified to a heart shot.

Mr. Wilson had barely returned to Junes' side when someone tried to open the door from the outside.

Cookies' remains prevented the door from opening. Before the visitor could start their insistent knocking, Mr. Wilson had yanked Junes' gun from his kneeling position and demanded.

"Who's there?"

"It's me! What's all the shootin' about?"

"Oh, Pete! Come around to the front door. June's in trouble and Cookie's dead."

"Holy crap! Hold on I'll be right there!"

"Can you stand, child?"

"Yes."

"Good! Get me the medicine kit from the bunkhouse."

Elsa ran out and Pete limped in from the other direction while Mr. Wilson stoically cut Junes' shirt sleeves down the seam so that when they moved him his shirt would stay behind.

"What in the name of Hell happened here?"

"That galoot over there attached us. That's all I know for now. Why don't you help Cookie? Maybe put him on the table. When I finish this I'll help you move that skunk out the door and dump him outside before

Elsa gets back. She shot him and doesn't need to be reminded of it."

Pete picked up the slight remains of the old cook and gently placed him on the table. Opening the door, he grabbed Al by his coat collar and hauled his immense bulk out the door without Mr. Wilson's' help.

He returned to help Elsa and Mr. Wilson bandage June. This was a considerable task because of the bulk of the fallen man. Passing the bandages around his back took all three and considerable effort. All three were standing around trying to figure out what to do next when Blackie pushed the door open from outside.

"That must be the fellow outside that I been trackin'."

"Trackin'? Where'd you pick him up?"

"Him and another rider had camped out at the swimmin' hole on Wolf creek. George and I picked them up there and I came to let you guys know they was in the area. George went off to tell the line camps."

"Too bad you weren't able to catch up with him before he got here. Well, now that you're here we might be able to get him in bed. Blacky, you and Elsa get the door from the shed to put him on and Pete and I'll bring one of the beds downstairs."

"We could put him in the bunkhouse?"

"No, he'll need lookin' after and you yahoos can barely take care of cattle and horses. We'll put him in here and Elsa and me can look after him. Get on now. Time's a'wastin' and we still have to get the doctor."

Chapter Fifteen

The morning was crisp and clear. A harbinger of winter bit into you from the wind but it still felt good. It wouldn't be long before it would hurt to be faced into the wind but for today the breeze was exhilarating. Made you feel alive when the day started. Spud meant to just ride straight up the valley to take a quick look before dropping over the ridge to spend the rest of the day traveling to the ranch and back.

While he could get by with the stores he had for a while longer, he couldn't stand not seeing Elsa any longer. It had been two week since she had left for the ranch and it was like she was still here. It was almost spooky. She was there in the morning and popped up all day long.

It would be good to put flesh and blood into her face again. She was probably all healed up now and anxious to leave. Spud could just picture her all antsy and impatient to be gone.

His daydream was starkly interrupted by a carcass down. Lying in an open glade was what could only be a cow. Spud approached slowly and dismounted when he got within twenty yards of what by now was obviously a young heifer that had been killed. He securely tied up both his mount and the packhorse and walked around the perimeter of the kill. She had put up a fight. Blood and hoof prints told of a long and viscous struggle but the prints also told of the inevitability of the outcome. Huge prints of a cougar were everywhere.

Singling out a clear one Spud laid his hand down upon it. The print extended almost three inches beyond his hand. Big cat! Spud strode up to the carcass and studied the signs.

The cat had feasted on the hindquarter and it was very fresh. The carcass was still seeping out blood from its many wounds. Spud surveyed the surrounding area. The tracks went uphill and into a grove of trees off to the right. That had to be where the cat had gone. He probably had lain around his kill until he heard the approach of the horses and fled up into the trees.

The excitement rose up inside Spud. The thrill was on and it felt great. A long time had passed since he had done any hunting and the remembrance of it was a physical thing to Spud now. It had to be done.

The young heifer would have given birth to ten cows in the next ten years at least. If you counted its' offspring's offspring, the ranch had just lost a hundred head in that time. More than they could afford. The cat must go.

Spud strode to his horses. They were already restless. They had been since Spud approached the kill. Spud checked their ties and retied both. Taking his saddle gun from the gray, Spud walked toward the trees. If possible he became more excited the closer he got to cover.

As he followed the sign of the big cat, his mind grew more inward and he could feel his surroundings as well as see them. He studied his breathing and let his fingers play on the rifle. It would not do to grip too tightly. Hard muscles were not ones that moved fast.

As he entered the tree line, the rifle was carried at his hip. The cat would either run or fight. If it chose to run he could get the gun up to take his shot, but if it decided to fight, the charge would come from the side. Accuracy was not at a premium.

He would be on top of Spud before there was time to move. Spud knew that swivel and fire was faster than lower, swivel and fire. The cat would be so close by then that he couldn't help but hit him.

A large rock outcrop rose up about thirty feet in front of Spud and it looked likely. Slow and steady were his movements as Spud moved into the clearing in front of the bluff.

Movement off to his left brought the rifle up and Spud saw the great cat leap onto the top of a large boulder. He settled, shifted his feet and sprung to a ledge about fifteen feet above him. Spud had already anticipated where he would jump to and had his sights set on the ledge before the cat even arrived. Slowly squeezing the trigger the bullet caught the magnificent animal behind the shoulder and threw him into the cliff. His body bounced off and catapulted down to the ground.

It was over in a heartbeat. The great cat, after many campaigns against his prey, had come to every living thing's reward. Spud knew there were not many who were his equal and spent some time just standing and looking at the crumpled body.

Finally moving, Spud set his rifle aside, drew his knife from his belt and crouched beside the great cat. Starting on his stomach and with practiced moves he began to remove his hide. One wall of the bunkhouse was covered in pelts and Spud took some pride that his would be the largest when he put it up there. Rolling the skin up Spud turned the carcass over and removed the bottom side.

With this job finished he gathered the skin and his rifle and walked back to the downed heifer. He decided that the underside hindquarter would be fine for human consumption and that the hide would make a good winter covering for the cabin window.

Spud took the leg and hide off. Wrapping the cougar's hide up in the cows' hide Spud shouldered the burdon and walked back to his horses. They could still smell the cougar even though it was wrapped up and put up a struggle before Spud could get the load tied down on the packhorse.

His plans would have to change. He would have to go the long way to the ranch since he would have to put the meat in the springhouse before it spoiled. That wasn't bad. He'd have a good story to tell and he wouldn't lose any more stock to the big cat.

Spud had staked the cowhide on the cabin wall to dry, put the rear quarter in the dank springhouse and proceeded down the trail toward the road when something happened in the corner of his eye. Couldn't tell what but it caused Spud to move the reins away from that side. The gray had indeed made a fine cutting horse. Just like June had predicted she responded to this almost imperceptible tug.

Spud was on the ground. His wind was gone and he lay there for forever to regain his breath. There was a nausea that replaced his whole being. He became the nausea. Too stubborn to pass out, he teetered between consciousness and going black for an eternity.

Chapter Sixteen

Stick had swung by the line shack to tell Spud that they were supposed to come in to the ranch house. George had said that there had been strangers around. The old man wanted everyone in. Not finding Spud he was on his way to the ranch.

Stick saw before him in a clear patch that gray mare Spud had cut out. She was standing in this clearing alongside the trail still saddled. They'd had people messing around and this did not look good. He let his mount pick the path and without moving his head surveyed both horizons. There was really only one direction from which danger could come.

The side of the trail that the creek was on held a clear open meadow for too great a distance to allow assault, if trouble was afoot it would be from those trees on this side of the creek.

Stick kept his gaze there as he got closer to the gray. Finally he could see the crumpled form of Spud a short distance from his mount and yes, there was something in that tree line. Might just be a bird but Stick didn't think so. He figured it would take more than a bird to fell Spud.

Without hurrying, he proceeded directly to Spud and dismounted on the side away from the trees. Of course he towered above the horse's back but at least it put up some barrier and it would shield Spud. He crouched beside the prostrate form and rolled him onto his back. To his surprise Spud was awake. "How bad are you?"

"Bad enough! They still up there?"

"Yeah. Saw some movement as I rode up. He's about half way up that tree line. Let me get a look at you."

Stick pulled his knife and sliced open Spud's shirtfront, Stick looked at a furrow in Spuds midsection bored out by the bullet's path. "Nothin' but a little scratch! What're you layin' around for?"

"'Fraid that fellow will try it again. Has the bleedin' stopped?"

"Yeah, it's starting to clot. Doesn't look like it's too deep either. You'll need a doc but I don't think it's bad. We just have to get out of this and you'll be fine. Listen, if I got you over to those rocks, could you sit up against them and cover me 'til I get around those trees and on his back side?"

"Do ya' think you can move me without breakin' it open?"

"Probably not but I can't see any other way. He should have taken a shot at me before I even got to you. Course I'se watchin' him the whole way but he didn't know that. He'll for sure open up if I try to get around him. He'd be trapped except to light out directly away from us if I get around him. Can you do it?"

"I can do anything if it's all I can do. Here let me hold on to your forearms and you pull. Better stay behind that mount."

"I'll walk him along beside us. Not likely to get a clean shot with him there."

Stick pulled Spud to the rocks. He stayed curled up so as to not stretch his wound out and it wasn't too bad. Stick carefully positioned Spud behind one rock and leaning against another, then pulled Spud's pistol out and handed it to him. How's that?"

"Fine! Where's he at?"

"Uphill from that big elm. Just in the fringe."

"Ok, but I can't hit him from here with a pistol!"

"Well, I ain't walkin' to your horse for the rifle. Just keep him there and with his head down. I've got to get across this open ground then it'll be just him and me on equal footin'. Can't see a skunk what's a drygulcher come out of that alive. You ready?"

Spud watched as the thin man swung one leg over the back of his horse and hung Indian fashion onto the side of him. He urged the horse into a run and was soon at full gallop toward the bend in the trail that would put him on the other side of the trees in which the murderer was hiding.

Spud watched intently for any movement from the area of the gunman, expecting him to try to shoot Stick's mount but nothing happened as Stick disappeared around the tree line.

Spud knew that the warm sticky stuff leaking into his crotch was blood. He felt his wound without moving his eyes from the target. The bullet had cut across his belly, not into it. Just a matter of how deep it had cut across to determine the damage it had done.

Maybe it was not deep enough to open up his intestines. That would more than likely mean his death so it had better not. It was the gray responding to the slight pressure when he spotted the movement that caused the miss. He would have to remember to kiss her and give her extra grain as a thank you.

Spud kept up his vigil for what seemed a long time. After what must have been an hour, a spat of gunshots broke the noonday stillness. Silence settled over the meadow for another long time. The tall redhead had better have won or trouble was still here.

An eternity passed before the redhead's horse broke out of the trees leading a horse with a body draped over the saddle. Relief swept through Spud as he waited for him to get down to him. Stick caught the gray's reins up and all three mounts pulled up beside Spud.

"Got the bushwhacker. Why he didn't run is beside me. He knew we was on to him when I did my injun stunt. I'd 'a lit out for the home fires about then if it was me. How you doin'?"

"Not bad! How the hell're we going to get me to the doctor?"

"Well, I could leave you here and go get the wagon or you can try to ride. Could you stay on?"

"No. I couldn't sit up. Hurts too bad. Maybe I could ride with you and you hold me up."

"Ride double? Want to try? If you can't we can always go get the wagon."

"If you can get me up there and hold me upright, I think it'll be fine. That wagon won't be much better what with all the joltin' around an' all. Why don't you find that big roan I brought for a packhorse and saddle him. He could carry double all day long?"

They had gotten Spud on his feet even if he couldn't stand straight. He was bent over beside the roan and Stick squatted down and put his head between Spuds legs and stood up. With Spud ridding on Stick's shoulders Spud was above the level of the saddle.

All he had to do was pull his butt onto the horse and balance himself while Stick pulled out from under him. "How's that feel?"

"I'm in one piece and not too painful but I can't straighten up! You're going to have to hold me on!"

"Hang on pard. I'll get up and get you to a bed."

Tying the reins of the three horses to the roan's tail, Stick got up behind Spud and set off down the trail.

It was beyond strange the picture they made. This lodge pole pine lookin' fellow with a stock of red hair that made him look like a skinny Christmas tree was ridin' across the prairie holdin' some galoot like he was a girlfriend. An observer not knowing the gravity of the situation would have died laughin'.

"Are you hurt too bad to talk?'

One look at his face all scrunched up like that would have told anyone that he was about to pass out but there was a "Hummh!" came out of him.

"Ok, well you don't have to say much, just listen. I promised myself to apologize and ask you to forgive me the next time I saw you, and I'm doin' that now. Just like June tol' me, I been lookin' at myself to see why I'm always mad and I figured it out.

I'm ashamed of the way I look. That's it in a nutshell. When you came in the bunkhouse I was thinkin' how you must think you're better'n me. I get to where I think everyone is makin' fun of me and sniggerin' behind my back."

"Wow! That's a mouth full! What're you goin' to do about it?" The pained expression had left Spud's face.

"I decided to do just what June said. I'll treat everyone nice and they'll like me. Then I can just go on workin' here and get along with everyone. What do you think?"

"I think it'll work. You've been treatin' me real nice lately and I'm startin' to like you a lot. Let me ask you this. If you're a real nice guy would that be enough to make you like yourself even if you ain't the best lookin' hombre in the world?"

"Maybe! I sure been likin' helping you out of this fix. Maybe that'd work. Maybe we could try that."

Chapter Seventeen

It took forever! Spud was balled up on top of the roan in the fetal position. That at least didn't pull the wound open. After a few miles the seepage down his leg stopped and only the jar of each hoof was felt in Spud's stomach. He'd endured that brand of agony for too long when Stick announced that he could see the ranch.

The pair with the cavalcade of horses trailing behind got all the way to the ranch house and still nobody hailed them. Sitting their mount, Stick yelled and still no one came.

The big redhead pulled his pistol out and fired a round into the soft ground. Within seconds Blackie poked his head out the door and acted as if the sight of their group surprised him.

"Are you two married now?"

"Oh, you idjit! Spud's been shot. Go get some help to get him down and don't take all day. We got to get him a doc."

The smile left Blackie's face, "Doc's here. I'll get some help!"

With that he disappeared into the house and could be heard yelling at the top of his lungs. Although neither man could tell what he was saying. In a very short time, Blackie arrived with George and a slightly built, and youngish man in tow. All three men got Spud down just as Elsa began barking orders at them from the porch. The entire way to a kitchen table was without question under her supervision. She was yelling unquestioned orders until they got Spud safely to the table.

It was almost worth getting shot just to hear the concern in her voice.

"Ok, young fellow, you're going to have to lie on your back in order for me to see. I know this is going to hurt but we have to see the wound."

Already seen it, Doc. Why don't we just take my word for it and I can stay like this?"

With a chuckle, "If you can operate on yourself, that'll be fine. But if you want me to do it, you'll have to turn over."

He helped Spud roll onto his back. While no sound arose, the agony on his face was felt by all three people as they crowded around the table. After spending an hour examining and cleaning the wound the doc straightened up.

"Not too bad! I don't think it's too deep. It just burrowed through the soft tissue and muscle without damaging the intestine wall, I think. I got it cleaned and open to the bottom of the wound. We'll have to watch for infection to be sure but I think you got off real lucky there cowboy.

I think what we'll do is put some loose bandages on to catch the seepage and leave it open to heal from the bottom up. We want to be careful that we don't get any pockets in there to fester later on. How does that sound to you?"

"It's about what we figured. If I can just curl up somewhere and sleep, I don't think I'll complain about anything."

"No, you can't do that. You'll have to stay on your back for a couple of weeks. It's very important to keep the edges of the wound from closing and let it heal from the bottom up. We got to get it started to heal from the very deepest part of the injury.

It won't hurt so much after you've lain on your back for a while. Most of the pain is caused by ripping open the part of the wound that had started to scab over. If you get it open you won't be tearing it anymore and you'll only feel the dull pain of an injury.

I'll give you something to take for the first few days, get you bandaged and in bed. I'm going to stay a couple of days to watch you and June and I hope to see both of you up and around by that time."

"June! What happened to June for God's sake?"

"Later! All in good time. Here take this."

∞

The realization that he couldn't swallow brought Spud fully awake. As he tried to work up some spit in the desert that had replaced his mouth, he saw that Elsa was beside him in a room with another bed in it.

"How you feeling, Spud? Can I get you some water or something?"

Without waiting for an answer and amid some unintelligible sounds coming from his bed, she pulled a dipper from a bucket sitting between the beds and bent to help Spud up for the water.

"Ohh! Wait a minute! Wait a minute. That just plain hurts. Why don't you put the dipper down and let's get me up first.

"Do you want me to get some help?"

"No, we can do it. Besides I come to see you not some smelly, old cowboy!"

"Oh, Spud, I thought you were dead when I saw you on that horse. I am so glad to see you like this I could lift you by myself."

She put her arms under his neck and lifted as Spud pushed himself up toward the head of the bed. After several small steps, he was more or less in a sitting enough position to drink. Elsa watched his face carefully as she held the dipper for him to drink slowly. "Why don't you let me get the medicine you need to take before you drink anymore?"

"Sure. Hey, June, isn't it a little late for you to be still hangin' around in bed?"

"A long story short, I got myself shot too. They're goin' to let me slack off for a while longer."

"You got shot too? What's goin' on around here?"

"Let Elsa tell you."

As she returned, "It was that damn Al Hartwig. He got into our kitchen and killed Cookie and shot poor June."

"Oh, must have been the other one that shot me!"

"Yeah, I looked. It was the one they called Wes that you and Stick killed. I sure thanked him a lot for saving you. And June sure saved me."

"Humm! That stuff the Doc gave me is workin' already. Tell me what happened."

"Well, I had just got up and went down to help Cookie with the fire and breakfast. As soon as I stepped into the kitchen he must have been there waiting for me.

He jumped out from behind the washroom and scared me to death.

Just the sight of him sent fear ripping through me. I never thought I could be that scared. He yanked Cookie out from behind the washroom door and started sayin' how glad he was to see me again. And, how he would rape me before he killed me just for old times' sake and stuff like that.

That's when June came through the back porch door to get his morning coffee. That skunk just turned and shot him. When he turned to shoot, Cookie charged him. He hit Al in the hand and saved June's life.

They struggled but Cookie was no match for that brute. I almost killed him before he could get Cookie but I was too late. By that time Mr. Wilson had come down to see what was happening and we got June bandaged up and sent for the doctor when Blackie and George got here. Then we no sooner got that done than you arrived to scare the life out of us again."

"Don't that beat all! Did he hit you hard June?"

"Bullet's in my liver the doc says. If I just stay still for a long time, it should be all right. But he didn't even give me any medicine like you. How you feeling?"

"Like all of us are lucky to escape this with only the outlaws bein' killed."

"No, Cookie's dead!"

"Oh, yeah! He was a nice old man!"

"Yeah, never even came too after that big ranny shot him. Hadn't of been for him we'd 'a all died. Kept that outlaw off Elsa till she shot him point blank.

If Cookie hadn't charged, the scum would have just shot me again and then killed both Elsa and him."

"Least-wise two of us made it to tell the story. Who knows he might have killed the Boss too. Wasn't long before he arrived. Never knew the old fart had it in him, but he sure came through when the chips were tossed in."

"Guess you never know till the pot's hot when the water'll boil. Not to be seen as selfish but I'm sure goin' to miss his pies!"

June's voice held deep felt emotion, "No, you didn't know him, I'm sure gonna miss him. He's been here forever and we spent every day together at least part.

Well, could'a been a lot worse. That big skunk was sure out on a kill. What got him so deadly, you know?"

Since Elsa had left to get the water bucket filled, "Guess it was Elsa. She sure gets men riled up."

"Don't I know that? Had me going. Might as well tell you before someone else does. I asked her to marry me a couple of days ago. Hope you don't hold that against me."

Maybe that bullet had hit his heart after all, "Why should I? You got as much right to love her as anyone. What'd she say?"

"Said that she liked me just fine but that she already had a man."

"But her husband's dead."

"Wasn't her husband you dumb cowboy. Said it was you. Don't you know?"

It was like he had been shot again, "No, I didn't." After a pause, "Said that did she? Well if that don't beat all!"

"How do you feal about her?"

"Yeah, I love her. Who wouldn't? What with the way she is. I just didn't know she felt the same way, is all."

"You better talk to her. Every man on this place is in love with her and ever one else that meets her is gonna fall for her. Might be she'll change her mind if you don't get it settled."

"Gosh, I can't believe it. I thought that I'd get her to California and that would be it. I'd never see her again. Why would she want a broken down cowboy?"

"Don't ask me! I think she should be after a' important foreman of some major ranch in the neighborhood. There's just no tellin' what a woman'll do. You look like you're about to pass out."

"Yeah, that stuff has me real groggy. Where's Elsa?"

Chapter Eighteen

She was sitting beside the bed in a rocker that someone had brought up for this purpose. Reading a book and sitting kind of sideways with a shaft of early morning sunlight beaming in that made her pretty enough to cry over. She could stop your heart she was so beautiful.

Spud was careful not to move and just stared at her. Could he be so lucky as to have her caring about him? He made up his mind to ask. Just come out and ask. That seemed best.

What if he couldn't work up the nerve and he lost what he had to have? June had said that was what she had said. So, he had to ask her.

What if she said yes? Wow, that would make an impression on his life. But then, he was already making room in his life for her, why not have all of her and really make way for her in his life? Sure sounded fine. He knew her sprit was pure and strong. And besides, why was he even arguing?

He knew that he would do anything for her that she wanted. He was already gone over her, wasn't he? His wound was still and not hurting much so Spud closed his eyes to sink into relaxation. When he opened them some moments later, he was looking flush into her deep brown ones.

"How do you feel?"

"Good really! Have you been up here long?"

"I spent the night here. Doc wanted to know if you were moving around in your sleep. Said we would have to tie you if you wanted to turn over. But you've been real quiet all night. I think I quit worrying around midnight and went to sleep. I woke up about three or four hours ago and you've been still since then too. Do you need some of your medicine or some water?"

"Let me see if I can sit up. Water sounds good and some coffee would be heaven."

She stood beside him while he slowly pushed himself up until his head was resting on the bedstead. "There I think I can drink now!"

He had the hot, black brew about half finished. Elsa had her hand on the bed's edge and was leaning forward in the rocker gazing at him. Spud placed his free hand over hers', "June said you told him I was your man."

"He did? Do you have a question to ask me about that?"

"Well, I need to know if you said that."

"Why would June lie?"

"Come on, you know what I mean. How did you know that I felt that way about you? I thought I was keeping it under my hat so you wouldn't feel uncomfortable around me."

"No, I've known for some time how you felt. You couldn't hide the way you feel about anything. That's one of the reasons you're so special. I just wasn't sure about what I was goin' to do about it until I left you. I think I was afraid you wouldn't want me after what those men did to me but I decided that you didn't have any choice. You were going to have me whether you liked it or not."

216

"Elsa, the truth is that ever' since June said that I've had a fire inside me. After I got to know the strength and courage and nobility you have I couldn't think of any other women. You're just the finest women there could ever be, but I never dreamed you would feel the same way about me. It was like my whole spirit exploded inside me when June said that. If you will, marry me and we'll make a life together that will make you as happy as anything."

"As soon as you can get up and around, I'll have the preacher come by. You'll have to promise me never to scare me like you did this time though."

"Oh, I promise! Oh, I'll take such good care of you!"

"We'll have to take good care of each other. It's not all on your back. I can take care of you too, you know. How would some food be?"

"That'd be great." Spud let his muscles relax as Elsa left the room.

"That was well done young man!"

Without opening his eyes, "You think I could do anything else? Make her more comfortable. I don't know a lot about what women want."

"Well, you're Ma must've trained you well, cause you did real good. You're a lucky man! Hope you know that and're prepared to treat her right."

Chapter Nineteen

Spud was stretched out on the veranda, dozing in the sun. His wound wasn't all healed but at least he could stretch out without the pain doubling him up. He was a married man now and you could see him grinnin' his whole life away. He looked like a damn clown, but a fellow couldn't rightly blame him if they took a look at his wife.

June had been moved into the bunkhouse and they had a room to themselves. They were going to take a ride as soon as Elsa finished up some figures she was recording in her elaborate bookkeeping book.

"You're lookin' awful peaceful this beautiful morning."

"If I get any more peaceful, I think I'll just naturally pass on over, Mr. Wilson."

"Well, it's a good thing I stopped to bother you. Wouldn't want to lose you after all this."

"No, sir. Need to hang around now that I have Elsa and all."

"Oh, I know. I don't care anymore of my own daughter than I do for her. Did I tell you that she has all my books done? Wants us to mark each cow and then she has a way to keep track of the animals that calve and how much it costs to raise them and what we get for them. Haven't done anything like that at all before.

She says that after a few years, we'll be able to get rid of the females that aren't producin' as well as the extra bulls. If that don't beat all? Never even needed to ask anyone how to do it either.

Just did it all on her own. Won't be the same when you two leave."

"Well, thanks Mr. Wilson. I know she thinks the world of you too. And, I do too. Sure want to thank you for takin' care of me like this."

"Not necessary to thank me. You work for me son. I count on you and you can count on me. All my men know that and now you do. I've been wantin' to talk to you some for a while now. That's really why I stopped by. Found out something maybe you ought to know."

"Sure Mr. Wilson. What's that?"

"Well, it's about Elsa and what happened at the line camp. Came into some knowledge about that and I figure you could better understand what a wonderful women you've got if you knew too."

"It's about Elsa?"

"Yeah. I heard part of the commotion that was goin' on in the kitchen. I was upstairs when there was a ruckus and I headed that way to see what was happening. When I got on the stairs, I could hear them screamin' at each other.

This outlaw scum and Elsa were goin' at it pretty good. He was sayin' how he was goin' to assault her and how much he was goin' to enjoy it, when she said somethin' strange. She said how she knew that he couldn't enjoy anything like that ever again. It was quiet for a spell, and then all hell broke loose.

That was when June arrived and guns started goin' off. He must have come in when there was that quiet spell. It bein' quiet in there he didn't know what was goin' on. What with the noise and smoke and June and Cookie I forgot all about what they had said.

Then a couple of days later Doc told me something he thought I should know. He had done an autopsy on the dead outlaw for the Sheriff. He has to have that before he can pay the reward. You know all about that. Anyway Doc says how this outlaw is missing part of his privates, if you know what I mean. Says that his major apparatus is mostly gone.

I put that together with what I heard and my respect for your little lady rose a great deal higher than it had been before I can tell you. What do you make of that?"

"If that don't beat all? Not that I had any idea of it but it sure don't surprise me none. There's been plenty of times when you couldn't help but notice the strength and courage of my wife.

I bet that was the reason he was beatin' her so bad when I got to the cabin. She said that she was sure they were goin' to kill her and that she wanted it to be soon rather than put up with what was happenin' to her. Probably felt that would help it along, and get even some too.

Sure glad I happened along when I did." After a pause, "Mr. Wilson, it might be better if we both just tell Elsa that we admire her a great deal without telling her why. She still hasn't gotten over what happened to her. Can't blame her much but it still bothers her something awful.

She's been getting' better since she killed him but bringin' it up to her would only make her feel bad, when we're trying to help her. If you could just tell her how you feel without mentioning the particulars, I would sure appreciate it."

"Didn't intend to mention it to anyone, young man. Not anyone's' business anyway. Not even Elsa's. This is just something I thought you should know. Wanted you to know that you didn't have any shrinkin' violet for a wife but a real thoroughbred. Should have known you already knew."

They sit in silence enjoying the slow warming of the early winter day.

Chapter Twenty

She was watching him as he saddled. He knew she was. She'd been watching his every move since he got hurt and he knew she meant the best. She was just seeing if she needed to help, but Spud made sure that he stood straight and tall. He could saddle a horse on his deathbed and he knew it. Still, it was a warm feeling to see the concern.

"You know we haven't talked about what we're goin' to do. Now that we're together our plans can change. I don't really need to go to California, and you said you were heading back to Texas back then."

"Yeah, I was. About the only thing that I knew that I wanted was to buy a place of my own. When I got the inheritance from Skinny I had enough to buy a little place and start working for myself. I was planning on Texas because I knew where I could get a herd by just rounding them up.

This place in East Texas has a lot of wild cows that haven't seen a brand since the Spanish come through way back when they were lookin' for gold. That's about as far as I had gotten."

They mounted and let the horses walk out of the yard. "It seems to me that with my money thrown in we could buy a herd or a better place. Which do you think is more important?"

"Um, probably in the long run a better place. In the short haul the quality of the herd but you'd always be limited by your land."

"Well, since we're young and plan on having' a family, I guess it's the land. What do you think of this land here in comparison to Texas?"

"The best places here are as good as the best places in Texas or better. The regular place I've seen in Nebraska are consistently better but the winters are a lot worse here. They must loose stock here that wouldn't be lost in Texas. Course we lose stock in Texas because of water that wouldn't be lost here. Probably evens out or they come out ahead here."

They came shortly to a large oak tree that set on the side of a hill by itself and pulled the horses up. They ground hitched them and loosened the cinches. Taking a blanket from behind Spud's saddle they stretched out in the shade. "You know the reason I'm asking these questions is because Mr. Wilson is going to sell Rafter. He told me a couple of weeks ago that he wanted to move to Cheyenne and spend what time he had left with his daughter and her children. Said it was getting' too hard on him to keep workin' this place and didn't want to put it all on June. What do you think of that?"

"News to me. He never said anything to me. I love this place. I think it would be as good as anything we could find anywhere really. Could we afford it though?"

"I don't know. He never said what he wanted but we've got a lot of money between us. We should be able to put enough together to get this. You said the banker would help you if he could."

"Yeah, never thought of that. Guess I just always paid for what I got or didn't get it. Is that what you want to do?"

"I'd sure love it here. These last few weeks have been the best of my life. Not just because of you either. I like this place. It's pretty and productive and the people are absolutely terrific."

Having said that, I'll also say that if you want to go to Texas, that's fine with me. We could find a good place down there and be happy for the rest of our lives but we better start decidin'. It's about time to get on with it don't you think?"

"How could you be so pretty and so smart at the same time? All the girls I knew before were either plain as vanilla and smart or pretty and dumb. How could you be so much of both? We'll have to decide!"

He drew her to him and kissed her with a gentleness and emotion he never knew he had. This planning sure stoked some fires in him. Must be a nesting instinct. He gently laid her over onto her back. He pulled back and looked directly into her eyes. "We'll talk later."

The warmth was leaving the suns' rays when the pair directed their mounts down from the hill. Seems they were spending a lot of their time out here. "You know, I think I'd like it here too. We'd never have to worry about the basics. Grass and water will always be here. We'd just have to care for our animals.

Maybe look after our deed when we become a state. That's something I was worried about in Texas. What with the talk of war and secession there, I'm not sure things will be stable for who knows how long. What say we talk to Mr. Wilson when we get back and see what he's thinkin'. Don't do no harm to see!"

"I think that's about the best we could do. Like you said all we'd have to do then is work from dawn to dusk but it'd sure pay off. Another thing I've been thinkin' about.

That's what kind of animals would be best. You know I told you that my ex-skunk was in the packing business back in Chicago. Well, they're starting to favor butcherin' animals that aren't these bony longhorns we're raising. There are several breeds that they're payin' more for than these.

My ex-Father-in-law's opinion was that the longhorn would be slaughtered for its hide and dog food before long. The amount of meat that the other breeds butchered down to would make the longhorn into a breed of the past.

Right now you can get ten cents a pound more on the hoof for two or three breeds of cattle than you can these. What do you make of that?"

"You mean sell off everything here and start a new herd?"

"I don't know what to do about that information. You would probably know much more about how to go about it than me. I just know what they're sayin' back east and I think you can be sure that it's goin' to happen if those men say it is.

They have power over the industry and we'd better take that into consideration. Young people have to be smart about what they do because things are goin' to change before they get old."

They rode in silence for a long way, "You're right about things changin'. Just since I was born, my Pa's workin' in the city at a job for wages. Not what he was doin' as I grew up. We need to be smart!

So, the best way to change the quality of your herd is through the bulls. You could sell off all the males and introduce what you wanted the herd to look like by buyin' new bulls. If you sold the old females as well as the males of each new generation, and bred the female hybrids with pure bulls, you would wind up with new cows without havin' to buy anything out of your pocket. Each purchase would be financed by what you sold from the last herd. Do you see what I mean?"

Elsa was impressed. "I knew you weren't just a pretty face, and the rest of you ain't bad either! That sounds like the way to do it. We could give almost all we have as down payment. Use the rest for operation expenses and borrow if we needed it at each purchase. Before we have a family we would be set to collect the benefits of all our planning. Let's not talk about it for a couple of days and see what we think then. If we still agree, then it's a go, all right?"

"All right!"

Chapter Twenty-one

The man getting out of the carriage drew attention. It was his size first. He was large. Real big around and real tall, but then you started to notice his appearance, probably more so than his size. Lots of men were as big as he was but not many looked like him.

His features had been hit too many times. The blows had forged a face not even a mother could love. It looked like lumps had broken out all over. His nose was as much like a bulldog's as the dog himself. His hands had obviously been broken many times. His knuckles were as big around as many men's wrists.

If you had known him around Chicago, you would know that he was indeed a man to be feared. His reputation for brutality was spread throughout the bars in that area. Most men sought out the weaker men to attack but not this guy. He wanted only the roughest to impose his will on and that had earned him a reputation spread far and wide. You walked the long way around Sam Schmidt.

He stepped lightly down from the carriage and tied up the two-horse set. With ponderous strides he moved toward a building that said Sheriff over the door, pulling open the door, he strode inside. "Lookin' for the sheriff."

"You found him stranger. My name's Thompson. What can I do for you?"

"I got a letter from you Sheriff. Said you might have knowledge of the whereabouts of a horse I've been lookin' for."

"Ah, sure! You must be Sam Schmidt. Glad to meet you, Sir."

They shook. "What can you tell me about the horse described on the poster? I got a client wants him back real bad."

"Sure, you're a Pinkerton man aren't you?"

Pulling his wallet, the big man spread out on the sheriff's desk two sheets of paper. "There you are Sheriff, my I.D. and the warrant for the horse. They's a description on the warrant and you'll see it's the same as the one on my flier."

The sheriff read both papers "Sure enough! Well, looks like you're who you say you are. Now this Black. We had a bunch of outlaws come through here raisin' hell. One of them was ridin' this Black. Had the brand on him and fit the description on your flier. Thought you might like to know. He's over to the stable. Want to go look at him?"

"Sure enough! I stand a good bonus to pull this big boy in. Like I said the owner wants him back real bad."

"You wouldn't happen to know anything about the gent what was riddin' him, would you?"

"No! Been followin' that horse since Chicago but never figured out who rode him. Always got information on the horse. People remember him, not who's on him."

They strode in silence across the street and down two blocks to the livery. "Hey Johnson! You here?"

Striding from the back, wiping his hands, "Yeah, What'd ya' want?"

"This here's Mr. Schmidt. Wants to look at that Black we put up in here."

"Sure. This way."

Leading toward a rear stall, "There he is! You the owner?"

"No, his representative. He sure will be glad to get him back. This boy's won a lot'a stake races all over the area back home."

Taking the animals head he pulled his lips back to reveal a tattoo on his upper lip. "See that, Sheriff? Same as what's on the warrant. Need anything else?"

"Not a thing. Looks like it's your horse all right. You'll have to sign some papers. You can come by any time after about an hour and we'll get it taken care of."

"Sure." Sam turned to the hostler. "If you'll get my buggy from the Sheriff's office and brush and feed my team, I'll pay the goin' rate." Seeing that he had been heard he turned and walked off to the saloon without waiting for a reply."

The stable owner whispered as the big man walked off, "You know who he is don't you?"

"Know his name if that's what you mean!"

"No, No who he is. That's a very famous man back east. I heard of him when I came through Chicago way back. Even seen him once. He's a killer. Kills men with his bare hands. Killed some of the roughest men in that big town, they all say."

"Uhmm, well, guess I'll just shoot him then if he gives me any trouble." The Sheriff turned and walked back to his office.

∞

"What'll it be?"

"Whiskey!"

When the barkeep put the shot down. "Know anything about that trouble around here?"

"Of course! Everybody knows about that! Biggest dust-up around here in many a moon. What have you heard?"

" Nothin'! One of them was ridin' my horse is all."

"That big, fast lookin' black?"

"Yeah, what happened?"

"This gang shot up the Rafter W and got killed for their trouble."

"You don't say! Any of the Rafter people get hurt?"

"Yeah! The foreman and a cowhand got shot but they're all right. Their cook got killed'. Recon they'll learn not to attack the Rafter!"

"Does sound like something everybody'd know about. Did they ever figure out what the outlaws wanted?"

"Not really! Some of the boys said they were after this woman all the time. Myself, I'm not so sure. Oh, she's a looker an' all but still. Seems like a lot a' trouble just for some woman, even one as pretty as she sure is. Ask me, I don't think we know all there is to know about it."

"Well, dead men tell no tales, uh?"

With a laugh, "You got that right. We'll never know the whole truth, you ask me."

"It's that way a lot in this old world. Know anything about the guy riddin' my horse?"

"Not really! His name was Hartwig. They say he was real large and the gal what did him in stands to collect a passel of money."

"None of that tells me anything. Say, what's the best place around for a meal and a room for the night."

"Both at the same place. That way to a big green house on the right. Says boarding house on the sign. Widder Horn will put you up and feed you the best food in town for next to nothin'."

"Guess I'll head that way. Might be back in after a nap and some food."

"Ok, see you."

The big man pushed the bat-wing door aside and strode out.

Chapter Twenty-two

Schmidt shouldered the door open and entered. The place had filled up in his absence. He was familiar with the inside of a saloon, since he had spent most of his adult life in one. Be good to get back home. At least there were women available there, not like this church ridden outpost. All the good folks took away what there was to enjoy in life. Didn't want anyone enjoying what they were denied he was sure.

Not only get back with some women but also he would be a lot richer than he was now if he could get this last bit of information without arousing suspension. He had carefully extracted what he knew from several different people.

Not one person in this town could put together all he knew about his purpose. Not much chance of even anyone trying to stop him much less succeeding in keeping him from his goal.

Soon he would put the last piece of the puzzle together and finish this rotten business up and get back home where he would be paid handsomely for all his effort.

He had been on the trail for three months, and he was close. All that was left was to work some goat tender in this bar and be done with it.

He chose a table in the middle of the large open room that had two men seated at a four-person table. "Anybody using this chair?"

"No, help yourself."

Schmidt lowered his bulk into the groaning chair, "Hey barkeep! Make it a shot and brew." He sat silently until the bartender delivered his order. Tossing back his shot and sipping his beer, he let his gaze flit around the room, making sure he did not look directly at his tablemates.

"You a stranger in town?"

"Not sure I'm all that strange but I never been here before."

With a chuckle the speaker offered, "Name's Kennedy. I'm a local farmer from out east of here."

"Glad to know you, Mr. Kennedy. Mine's Schmidt and I'm just passin' through. I've been on the road for a while."

"Guess that gets old fast. Where you from?"

"Does! You gents need another?"

After they were served. "Out of Chicago. Been tryin' to track down a horse that was stolen back there."

Schmidt let the conversation run along general lines while keeping the glasses full. As the evening wore on the effects of the alcohol began to be apparent.

His companions at the table were so glassy eyed that they would never be sure they had even been asked the question much less answered it. "Say gents, I been thinkin' that it would be a good idea to ride out to the place where my horse was found. Might be they know some about the gent what was ridding him or at least I could thank them. Either of you know where this place is?"

"Sure! It's just off the road to Cheyenne. You go down to the Cheyenne road and head west. After you go across the creek, you'll see a trail leadin' off to the right that goes to the old Warren place. You keep goin' another three or so miles and take a track leading off to the right. That'll take you right up to the ranch house. Can't miss it."

Schmidt let the conversation go on for a while longer and then said, "Guess I'll be gone, gents. Got to get started back early tomorrow. Chicago's a long way off. Good to meet ya'!"

"You bet! Take care of yourself and see you some other time."

The big man made his way out of the bar and back to the boarding house.

∞

Early morning found him sitting on his bed checking his guns. Not a western rig. He had two holsters, one under each arm. The big forty-fives didn't look like a typical cowboy's either. That was all right with him.

He was sure these punchers were not his equals in any way. Back in Chicago they would get eaten alive and then spit out. Well by mid-day he would have this finished, might even have some people dead by then. Depended on what he found.

One thing he was sure of was that no one would stand between him and his goal. He had put many a man in the ground for even considering it. Not a soul in this neck of the woods could stand to him.

He finished the job to his satisfaction and went to find the holster at the stable. Need to shake the dust of this dump out of his system. "Get my horses taken care of?"

"Sure! You pullin' out?"

"Yeah. Get the rig ready and I'll pay you off when I get back from the Sheriff's."

After walking the short distance, "Mornin' Sheriff. Got those papers ready?"

"Sure! Here you go."

The big man bent over the desk to sign where indicated. "Been with the Pinkertons long?"

"No! Is that all ya' need?"

"Um, need to fill in that blank for the real owner's name."

That's the real beauty of this whole thing the killer thought. No need to lie about anything. With that warrant in his pocket for the woman, this whole thing was legal. From the horse to what he was about to do to the women- it was all legal.

He wouldn't even have to apologize for dead bodies left in the wake of doing his duty as an officer of the law. They would be hindering an officer enforcing a warrant. Besides, he would be hard to find.

He wasn't even a Pinkerton. The old man had given him those IDs when he hired him for this task. The paperwork was all real though. Sam guessed that his employer had enough pull with the Pinkertons to get him hired temporarily for his purposes.

The sheriff tried again, "Know I asked you afore but you come up with any idea where the hombre ridin' your horse got him?"

"No!"

"Just seems strange that this gang from Missouri and Arkansas would wind up mounted on a bronc stolen in Illinois is all. Figured you might have found on their back trail where they come upon that mount."

"No! Like as not they came upon the gent what stole him and killed him for the horse. All I done was send out the fliers and wait for a reply. Like you sent notice to me. I been all over lookin' for info on him but I never got close to who was riddin' him."

"Yeah! All that makes sense but still seems that something is missin'. Who was the gent that contracted with the Pinkertons to find him?"

"Never met the man, Sheriff. Heard he was an old man that was rich as all hell but that's only heard. And not from too sharp an observer if you ask me. Might be he's just some sodbuster with a race horse."

"Yeah, you're probably right. Still it's mighty strange! Like you for instance. Seems like a man like you wouldn't be sent traipsin' all over hell's green acres lookin' for some horse. As I hear it you got some reputation back east and might be expected to occupy your time with more important matters."

The inattention left the big man. "Told ya' it was a good payin' job. Besides you let me worry about what I make."

"Yeah, sure. It's just that it's my job to worry about makin' things make sense. Sometimes they just don't though."

"If that's all you need?"

"Sure. We got it taken care of. Thanks Mr. Schmidt."

"Thank you Sheriff. Without you, I'd still be out there beatin' the bushes."

Maybe these country bumpkins weren't as dumb as they looked. That Sheriff was doing some heavy thinking. It was too late though. If he ever put it together it would be after it was all done and Schmidt long gone.

Chapter Twenty-three

George and Stick had the pump blades loose and were lowering the gear and box down to Spud waiting on the ground. They would have to replace a drive gear that had been busted for almost a year and then put it back up there on the windmill.

Spud hated grease. Got on your hands and then on your rope and reins and everywhere. Good to be the owner and choose what job you got to do. Spud watched as the two cowpunchers with grease up to their elbows let the rope play out in their hands. The assembly lowering to Spud's gloved ones.

Get it into the wagon and the job would be done until they were back at the ranch house where Pete could take the gear assembly box apart and put a new gear in it then.

Spud and Elsa had owned this spread for the better part of a week and all was well. Spud had already learned to love the place. Mr. Wilson was still here and would be for the foreseeable future. He was waiting to buy a home in Cheyenne across from his daughter, and having him around added a lot to the new experience.

Spud had talked to Skinny for countless hours around a campfire about what it would be like to own their own place. They had mapped it all out in their minds and swore to someday make it come true. Skinny wasn't here to enjoy it but Spud knew that if he had been he would have approved.

Having the place be made up of Skinny's boyhood home would make him awfully proud, and somehow made him a part of this place. Being married to the most beautiful and best women in the world was what made it the most important. If he had known how happy it would make him, he would have hunted down Elsa years ago and forced her to marry him if necessary.

The boys were a terrific outfit. He already knew them from having worked with them and knew he could count on them and that they were accomplished cowhands.

June it turned out owned the land around the widow range line shack. Seems he had homesteaded forty acres around the buildings and then had others homestead around that and bought it from them. One hundred and sixty acres were his now along with part of the herd they had been working on the Rafter.

He had decided years ago to take part of his salary in cattle and now had a sizable herd. He had decided not to join them in their makeover of their herd and was going to spend most of his time at the line camp.

It seems he was of a mind to asking a lady in town to join him there. Spud was surprised to learn all this but was also very pleased. The big foreman would continue to work for Rafter during roundup and trail and now had two hands employed at his place.

It was just all coming together so well it made the whole situation dreamlike. Life could be sweet if they could only get this unit repaired and back up pumping water.

Stick called from the platform, "Someone's comin'."

"Can you see who it is?"

"Naw! Rides like a tenderfoot, though. Flops all over the place, and he's comin' fast."

Spud walked over by the wagon to be close to his rifle. "See anything yet?"

"Yeah, looks like Pete!"

"Pete! What the hell's he doin' here?"

"Yeah and what's he doin' on the back of a horse? Not supposed to be doin' that for another month."

The two on the ground could see him now. He was coming on at a pace too fast for his still broken leg. He had one foot out of the stirrup and that was what caused him to look like a novice. They all three watched him as he slid his mount to a stop close to the wagon.

"What's all the rush?"

"All hell's broke loose! Some yahoo hit Wilson over the head and took Elsa."

Took Elsa? Where?"

"Don't know. He was on that black the outlaw was ridin' and took off down the road. Figured I could never catch him with this leg and so I got the idea to come here."

Stick growled, "What the hell's that goin' to do? You should've stopped the bastard!"

"Couldn't have. They were gone by the time I got up to the house but I been thinkin'. They could be cut off from town by a fast horse cutting across country through the gorge.

Stick and George could take off after them down the road and Spud could put that gray across country. If any horse can make it in time, she could."

"What cross country?"

"The road to town's over there." Pointing off to the Northeast. "Reason we don't go that way is this gorge that runs between here and the road. You'd never get a wagon through it but you can take a mount that way 'cause there's a' old game trail down into and out of the gorge a horse can get through.

You just keep on after that and you'll come to the town road just before it crosses the river. Could be it'll get you there before that kidnapper gets there. They only got about a thirty-minute head start on you. Had to bandage up Mr. Wilson's head. Stop the bleedin'."

Spud stood for only a second. "Good plan! We'll follow it! You two stop at the ranch and get extra horses and provisions. Then take out after them. I'll try the gorge. If they went that way, maybe I can stop them. If not I'll catch up with you goin' in the other way.

If they went toward town and I'm too late to stop them we'll keep after them in that direction until we get him. Where is this trail through the gorge?"

Stick, who had slide down the ladder and caught up his and George's horses as Pete talked, spoke up. "See that bald knob stickin' up over there? Head just to the north of it and that'll bring you out on a' open space with a big pile of rocks in the middle.

You'll need to find a big solitary elm tree to the left of those rocks and head for that. You'll see the cut in the bank from there and go on through. When you get to the other side head due east and you'll see the road in about a mile."

Stick and George had already pulled out as Spud ran to catch up his mount. "You take it easy on the way back, Pete. No sense in you getting' hurt! An' take care of Mr. Wilson 'til we get back."

He pulled the cinch tight and vaulted into the saddle. Pointing his horse in the right direction he urged her to a run. Carefully coaxing her to more and more speed, Spud made sure he was relaxed and concentrating on helping her with her rhythm.

Within a quarter of a mile the horse and rider were burning the wind. She was flat out and the rider was bent over to offer less wind resistance. With each leap, Spud's mind became more terrified. Keeping in rhythm with the magnificent animal, he decided it had to be something to do with her past. The father of her dead husband probably.

That meant that they aimed to kill her at some point. She was dead if they failed to rescue her, either at their hands now or back in Chicago. He hoped it was the latter, because he knew they would never get to Chicago. Not as long as he drew a breath.

With that decided, all of his attention went to aid the speeding horse. She had turned into a machine, beating the ground with a speed and fury that only a great athlete could produce. Spud was almost lost in awe of this performance when they burst out on what had to be the open space.

He pulled his animal in and studied the terrain ahead as the gray kept at a less frantic run. There was the tree and as they neared, Spud slackened their pace even more. He guided her up to the bank and jumped off. Leading her down the cut bank, carefully picking the way down the narrow and precipitous trail and up the other side took too long.

Jumping aboard on the far bank he slammed her into a run again but the climb had taken something out of her. The rhythm was wrong. Spud tried to help her get the pace but it wasn't getting better. A flat out three mile run was a lot to ask of any animal and she might not make it.

Despair started to grip his heart. He could feel it tighten until his breathing became difficult. For the first time in a long time he did something desperate. His spurs had only been used to stay aboard a bronc before now but he applied them to his gray. He started low and raked her sides long and hard. Her head jerked up and she startled out for several strides but as her stride leveled out again her head stayed up. She steadied out after that and the wind swept past the fleeing pair in great gulps.

Her second wind had arrived and she was an animal to behold. Spud felt for the first time that they would make it. He settled down to aid her in her run to save Elsa.

Her stride remained strong and constant until Spud's touch reined her to guide around a spine of trees and came out in view of the town road. There was a spire of dust rising back up the road to his right and he was sure that was his quarry. He had to drown the tide of excitement arising in him.

Studying the road, Spud decided that the best place to meet him was around a curve in the road. He could station himself so that when the kidnapper rounded that curve Spud would be too far away for pistols and just right for his saddle carbine. The outlaw wouldn't have a chance.

Spud had already decided to shoot him without giving him a chance. Better to not give him a chance to hurt Elsa. Whoever he was he wasn't going to get much older.

Spud reined down the grey in stages. By the time they arrived at their destination she was at a slow trot. Directing her to the middle of the road, Spud dismounted and palmed his saddle gun. Wrapping the reins around the saddle horn so she could keep walking until she cooled some, Spud smacked her on the rump and squatted in the road to wait.

He concentrated on making his breathing steady out while he looked carefully around. Satisfied that all was as it should be, he moistened his finger and whipped the sights on his rifle to remove any dirt or lent.

Dropping to one knee he presented a deadly picture to anyone moving down the road. A two-team buggy with the black tied to the tailgate and Elsa on the passenger side came into view almost before he was ready.

He swung the rifle up and took out the slack on the trigger. Before he could get the sights steady on his target, the big man on the seat made a catlike move that saved his life for a short time.

With amazing speed and agility, he just fell off the wagon. A lesser man would have broken his neck. The big man showed what had kept him alive in his rugged life. Like a ball, he rebounded from the roadbed before his body stopped its slide. Like a cat he managed to grab the side of the wagon before it got past him.

Keeping his feet under him, he walked his hands one over the other, letting the wagon pull him along with it. Always keeping the wagon between himself and the crouching Spud, the big outlaw got to the tie rope on the Black. Still letting the wagon pull him along he carefully untied the big horse.

Spud held his sights on him as he went through this astonishing play but held his shot. The wagon shielded him for a complete shot so Spud kept his rifle on him and waited.

When the outlaw yanked the reins out of the knot, Spud expected him to flee away from him. In that instant he decided to shoot him in the back.

It was in that instant that Spud's convictions changed forever. Older, wiser heads had always argued with him that if you become convinced that something wanted to hurt you, you had to kill it. Be it man, animal or object you showed respect until your life was at stake and then you kill it without mercy. He had never believed that.

Now, with someone else's life at stake, he could see the need for that. If it was just him, the outlaw could have gone but not with Elsa involved. The big man would die even if he fled, but the big warrior fooled him.

Leaping upon the black, he showed what had kept him winning fights all these years. He spurred his mount and charged straight at Spud. Racking the horse cruelly with his spurs he pulled both big guns from his armpits and started shooting them.

Spud had chosen his distance carefully and the bullets fell far short of him. Even as the man from Chicago raised the trajectory of his shots there was little chance of him hitting anything, while Spud took careful aim on the on-charging man. The heavy slug caught Schmidt high in the middle of his chest and blew him flat against the horse's back. His body balanced there for several bounds and then sagged to the side and fell. It bounced once and settled in the dusty road facedown.

Spud knew he was dead and his attention immediately shifted to Elsa. The team pulling the wagon hadn't let all the commotion bother them. When their reins went slack they continued their pace for a time then slowed to a walk and now they were walking quietly toward the fallen figure with Elsa bound on the seat.

Spud jumped to his feet and ran toward the wagon. He charged past the prone shape without a glance and grabbing the reins of the team, he tied them off. Spud chucked the rifle into the wagon and lifted Elsa down from the seat. Clutching her to him, he started to sob helplessly.

"I'm all right! I'm all right!"

"Oh, thank God! Thank God!"

"Darling, you're hurting my arms."

"Oh, I'm sorry! I'm Sorry!" Setting her on her feet, Spud began to untie her arms bound behind her back. "Is anything hurt?"

"Calm down, darling! You need to calm down. I'm all right. He didn't do anything to me except tie me up. Is Mr. Wilson alright?"

"Yeah, Pete said he was ok."

"Oh, thank God. I thought he had killed him. The big brute hit him so hard. It looked like his head was busted open."

"No, Pete said he had to bandage it up but that he was fine. I told him to go back to the ranch and take care of him until we got back. You sure you're all right?"

Grabbing him around the neck and crushing him to her, "I'm fine, you wonderful man! How did you get here?"

"It was Pete's idea. That owl hoot shouldn't have left him alive. He came up with the idea of ridding out to where we were working and having us take off across country and head him off. That idea worked real well, thanks to that mare over there. She was magnificent. You should have seen her on the run. We owe her for your life. Let's sit down."

Guiding her to the roadside he sat down under a tree to hold her in his arms for a long time. "Who was that guy?"

"He was hired by my father-in-law. Said he had followed the black and then figured out who I was."

"Well, it was sure close! Too close!"

"I was sure trying to figure out what I could do. You know, he said he had a warrant for me!"

"Really? That old man must have some pull. We better check him for papers. We don't need anyone else seeing those."

"Yeah, look in his pockets and I'll look in his bag."

They both sped to their appointed tasks. Spud turned him over and went through his pockets while Elsa went through the bag on the wagon. They both came up with papers and retired to the tree again to inspect them.

"Here's the warrant on you and one that says the black was stolen and this guy has the right to recover him. Says he's a Pinkerton"

"These are all letters from my ex-father-in law agreeing to pay him twenty a day with a bonus of five thousand for the horse and ten thousand for me. Never knew I was worth that much."

"Well, what are we going to do? Will he just send someone else after you?"

"How's he going to know that his hired killer is dead? We could just plant him and let the old goat wonder what happened to him."

"That'd only work if he wasn't keepin' anyone advised of his whereabouts."

"Yeah. We could check in town to see if he posted any letters or sent any telegrams. Wade would tell us."

"Sure he would. That'd tell us a lot but we can't just bury him. Too many people already know about him. We'll have to take him in. Could get bad."

"Well, we'll just have to do the best we can. If the worst happens we can still run. Go on out to California. They'll never find you there."

"All right! We'll just have to see what happens and do the best we can to help things along. How long before the boys'll be here?"

"Probable in the hour."

"We'd better take care of the mare and catch the

black. Don't want anything happenin' to her after what she did today."

They had everything done and had been sitting in the shade for a while when Stick and George turned the corner in the road. "Well, looks like you made it. Everything all right?"

"Yeah, she's fine. He didn't hurt her only tied her up and threw her in the wagon. How's Mr. Wilson?"

"Looks bad. Pete was goin' ta throw him in the wagon and bring him to town for the doc to look at. Who was this ranny?"

"Not really sure. Probably someone hired by Elsa's ex-father-in-law. That's not something you can share with anyone else and it's a fact we want knowledge of all this to stop here if we can."

Sure, boss. 'Nuff said! What're we goin' to do with him?"

"Help me load him into his wagon and we'll run him into the Sheriff."

"You think that's best? The sheriff's goin' to do his job!"

Ol' Stick wasn't as dumb as he looked, "Not any choice. Too many people know about him now. We'd never be able to keep the cat in the bag. Best to play it straight and see what happens. Keep as much above board as we can and put out fires when they start."

"Well, Boss, far from me to argue but only Mr. Wilson and people who work for you know about him and I for one would swear to not tell anyone."

"Me too!"

"Boys thanks! That means a lot to both of us to have you sidin' with us, but what do we do about the wagon and the black?"

"You're goin' to Denver next week. You could take them and sell them there. The horse belongs to you anyway, don't he?"

"Yeah! Well at least to Elsa. I tell you what, let's load the body and wait to talk to Mr. Wilson and Pete before we decide. How's that sound?"

"We better get the buggy off the road. Someone else's likely to come along."

Chapter Twenty-four

Sam Wilson squirmed around until he found a more comfortable position on the bench. They had moved the benches a month ago as the season changed and Sam was enjoying the early morning sun. Everybody in town (at least the males) hung out here to while away the time and the evidence was obvious.

On the ground at his feet were the shavings from countless whittling and tobacco stained the packed dirt. The rules of the bench area were, tobacco cuds had to be spit out where people could not step on them but spit could be anywhere except onto people. The general store owner had tried to instill some manners by putting a spittoon beside the bench but his efforts fell on unresponsive heads. The men had left the house to get away from their wives' house rules not to acquire more mannerly habits.

Sam was sure that town living wasn't going to be bad. He had spent three days in town now and was just waiting for the Doc to pronounce him fit. The headaches from being pistil whipped had subsided and the wound itself had quiet hurting and almost healed. When the Doc said travel was ok, Elsa and Spud were to take him to his new life in Cheyenne. You sort'a traded animals for people when you moved from the ranch to the city and Sam was beginning to think that conversation would be welcomed change.

The new hotel was clean and well-ordered and you had plenty of time to think. Cheyenne was even going to be better with those two youngsters to get to know. Still the open range was something that left a hole when it was gone.

Sam wondered what he would do after living in the open skies for so long a time. He could always make arrangements to keep contact. He sure had enough money to make a place out here he told himself. Maybe put a house somewhere? That bluff over by Skinny's folks place would be a view and a half. He made a note to talk to Spud and Elsa. Maybe he could have the best of both worlds. Bring those young boys out here once in a while. Teach them about cowboyin'.

He had settled himself on the bench shortly after finishing breakfast and reading the local paper. He had been building pipe dreams the rest of the morning. Just figuring things out and enjoying the early morning bustle of the town while being by himself.

The usual crowd that was always hanging out here to enjoy talk about weather, range conditions and what everyone else within a forty-mile circle was doing hadn't materialized yet. As the chill of early autumn was turning to a comfortable mid-morning, a familiar figure pushed the door to his office closed and strode in Sam's direction.

"Hey there, Old Timer! How's that head?"

"Still got a little ache. Doc says as soon as that's gone he'll cut me free."

"Could have told him that we done run several scientifical experiments on the subject and discovered that neither of us got anything in our heads what can be hurt."

"Ain't that the gol-darned truth? That's why I stuck it out there so's it could take the brunt of the blow. Didn't want my arms to get hurt."

"You ever goin' to tell me just what happened to you? Seems since I'm still sheriff, I might need to know."

"No! Ain't goin' to have you laughin' at me for the rest of our lives. Besides, I look stupid enough with this bandage on without actually bein' stupid enough to get this done to me."

"You ask me, you're damn lucky to walk away from this one as old as we're getting'. Ain't neither of us what you'd call spry anymore. Could have been your end from the way you looked."

"Ahhh! Like you said, ain't nothin' to be hurt up there. Though we both are leavin' it to the kids, uh?"

Yeah. Noah's goin' to be deputy for a month then take over. Town's goin'a let me stay in the Rolph place for as long as I live. Give me a little pension. Guess I'll do a lot of fishin'."

"You still goin' to spend part of the year with me, ain't you? We'll show those old gents at the cattleman's club how to play cards."

"Sure! Far's I'm concerned, it'll be good for both of us. Lookin' forward to it. Did you ever see life getting' like this?"

"I's thinkin' this very morning how the world has slowed down on me. Why when I was these youngsters age that are takin' over for us I'd be up at five and be antsy by six-thirty about why we didn't have everything done that I planned on doin' that day.

If I hadn't had June to stand between me and the men, I'd have run all my help off. Now, ten's fine to get started. Takes about that long to decide what's best to do and then work up to getting' started.

Speakin' of June, did I tell you he's goin' to stay on his place 'cept for spring and end of summer work. Spud and him's goin' to separate their herd and work independent like."

"Yep, you told me. I think him getting' married is even bigger news."

"How'd you find out about that? Just been last week."

"Mrs. Johnson told me. I been hangin' around her tryin' to spark her for a long time now. Even though I could be her grandfather, I had my hopes. You never know unless you try.

So she told me. Just to keep me away probably or maybe we're friends. I can't tell anymore. Tell me what the hell got into June. Can't see him even bein' able to talk around a women."

"It was that girl's fault. He went crazy over her as soon as she came to the ranch. Tried every way he could think of to get her to take after him. She set him down and explained how he was an attractive man and all but she had someone else.

I don't think June ever thought of himself as bein' anything but ugly. What with his bein' like he is. Elsa convinced him how a powerful man that was still gentle and thoughtful was what brung the cows home and damn if he didn't start to buy it after Spud came down. Them two talked for hours on end when they were in that room hurt you know. After that, ol' June had a fire built in him.

Went to town as soon as he could ride and came back with the Widder Johnson as his betroved. Beats all I ever' heard of."

"That girl, uh? I can see that. She lights a fire in me ever time I get to see her. I can sure see how she could stir things up some."

"You never seen anything like her, I'll tell you right now. She's not just good lookin'. They's something about her. A nobleness of spirit. She's a fighter in the old sense. Like the old days. Reminds me of the Paynee a few years back. Yet, she's pure as a angel and smart as anyone I ever knowed.

Them two's got it all figured out how to change the entire herd around and a lot of it came from her, I'll tell you. She know's a lot and wouldn't back down from a grizzly."

"What's this about a herd?"

"Oh, you should have heard them two. They'd sit around the house and talk for hours on end about what they would do. I couldn't get enough of eavesdroppin' on them. It beat all I ever heard.

With me and Moon, if we came to an impasse where we couldn't agree, well then it'd be done my way. I'as the man and we'd do it my way, even if it was the wrong way. Not those two youngsters.

They'd argue and try to change each other's minds until one would say, "Well, let's sleep on it. You think about it and we'll talk about it next Saturday." With all I knew of the young man, I found it hard to believe he was less than a man. He'd stood up against big odds several times since I knowed him but still that skirt was pushin' him around.

Well let me tell you they kept workin' things out and I kept watchin' and finally it dawned on me. To them it was more important to get it right than it was to win.

They were doing what everyone ought to do. I think about Moon and me and what it would have been like if we had known that. With her bein' Indian and all, she was as bad as or worse than me. She would have thought I was a squaw and left me probably if I had let her win an argument.

We could have done it these kids' way, the way we felt about each other would have been special. I know she held grudges when I rode roughshod over her.

You know plenty of times when she was thinkin' of puttin' a knife in my back, I'll lay. I'd 'ave felt better if I could've respected her enough to say she was right when she was.

These kids have made me look back now and see how it could have been so much better. What we gave up to keep doing things the way our parents had done them. How simple it would have been if only we had used our minds and how much better we could have made our lives together.

Not that we weren't happy- we were. You know how much I loved Moon, but we could have been so much better if only we had tried to figure out our own way like these kids have. It's sad that so much of the time we humans just keep on goin' the same way like lemmings over the cliff without even tryin' to figure out a better way."

"Damn, when was the last time you strung that many words together? You really been thinkin' on this haven't you?"

"You bet! That's all I been figurin' out since I met those two. Don't you think they beat all?"

"I'll say! It's that same thing I been tellin' you for years. They's doers and then they's thinkers. Thinkers are the most important by far.

You been arguin' for just as many years that you favored the doer. Can't you remember your sayin' "Don't think it to death, do something!" Now you see that I's right all along. Just like I am about everythin' else."

"Oh, yeah. Course that'd a' been the only thing I learned from you in all these years. By the way, they're goin' to change the longhorns over to blooded stock."

"What's wrong with what they've got?"

"They say the longhorn's no good. They've decided on an English breed called Hereford. What they plan is to sell all the bulls next spring and put Hereford bulls out. They're going to take me to Cheyenne and then go to man just north of Denver and purchase their stock for delivery next spring. Then go on to Denver for a Honeymoon.

They'll cut out the old longhorn heifers after they've calved early next spring and drive them to a spur on the railroad north of here. Get almost enough to pay for the Herefords.

Next year they'll start culling out characteristics of the longhorns and have a new herd in two years."

"Sounds like that'll work. Why they doin' it, though?"

"Elsa says that they can get ten cents a pound on the hoof more for them in Chicago when they're Herefords. Not only that but in a few years they won't even be butcherin' Longhorns except for their hides. The meat they get from a butchered Hereford is just so much more than from a longhorn that the longhorn will die off.

They plan on getting' a spur built up north on the railroad and having railroad cars dropped there to fill with their cows and anyone else's who wants to join. That way they can sell directly to the meatpackers in Chicago for a lot more money."

"I seen what they're talkin' about at the fair in Cheyenne. They're awfully short compared to longhorn. And, how they goin' to make it through our winter?"

"Elsa says to look at the muscles. That's your meat. She says we do too much lookin' at the animal. We want a big brute, while the slaughterhouse, our customer, looks at the meat.

As for the winter, they're buying theirs from a gent that's been raisin' them in the mountains for several years. I tell you, I think they're right.

You should talk to folks around here and let them know. Maybe some of the ranchers can see the writin' on the wall and will join them. Could save them a lot of trouble in a few years."

"You know the people around here. They got to see it to believe it, but I'll be glad to talk it up. Maybe someone will join them. Better chance in a couple of years when folks see if it pans out."

"Yeah! You're probably right. God that sun feels good!"

www.ingramcontent.com/pod-product-compliance
Lightning Source LLC
Chambersburg PA
CBHW060530260626
47161CB00003B/841